A special thanks to the wonderful people of the
Pacific Islands for inspiring us on this journey as
we bring the world of *Moana* to life.

randomhousekids.com

ISBN 978-0-7364-3574-1 (hardcover)
ISBN 978-0-7364-3600-7 (paperback)

Printed in the United States of America

10 9 8 7 6 5 4 3 2 1

DISNEY
MOANA

The Deluxe Junior Novelization

Adapted by Suzanne Francis

Random House 🏠 New York

Chapter 1

The old tapa cloth, made from the bark of trees, had a simple image of the ocean painted across it. For the audience of the story, the waves seemed to come to life in their imagination each time the storyteller told the ancient tale.

"In the beginning, there was only ocean," the storyteller said as the little waves rose and fell, "until an island emerged: the mother island, Te Fiti."

Upon the tapa, the listeners could almost see the appearance of an island goddess, rising up from the ocean and growing in size as the storyteller continued. "Her heart had the power to create life itself. And she shared that power with the world." The lovely goddess lay on her side, the curves of her body becoming mountains and valleys. It appeared to be the birth of a perfect world. A spiraling heart blazed at the very center of the island and a force radiated from it, sprouting beautiful trees and plants.

"But in time," the storyteller continued, "some began to covet Te Fiti's heart, believing if they could possess it, the heart's life-giving power would be theirs alone." A variety of wicked creatures appeared below the image of Te Fiti, eyeing her heart. "And one day, the most brazen of them all voyaged across the vast ocean to take it."

A small boat appeared upon the tapa, sailing across the rippling waves with a giant man, full of muscles and carrying a fishhook, at the helm. The man jumped off the boat, leapt into the sky, and magically transformed into an enormous hawk. Soaring through the sky, the hawk flew toward the lush island of Te Fiti with great purpose and determination.

Once it landed on the island, the hawk turned into a chunky green lizard. It quickly and quietly scampered through the dense foliage, its tail slithering behind. When it reached large rocks, it transitioned into a tiny bug to remain unseen and squeezed between them. The bug emerged on the other side and turned back into the man. Behind the shadows, the man anxiously eyed the spiral surrounding the pulsing heart at the island's center.

"He was a demigod of the wind and sea," said the storyteller. "A trickster, a shape-shifter with a magical fishhook. And his name was Maui."

Gripping his enormous fishhook, Maui stuck its point beneath the heart and pried it from the spiral. He proudly flipped it into the air before catching it. Then, to Maui's surprise, the ground began to shake.

"Without her heart, the island of Te Fiti crumbled, giving birth to a terrible darkness," the storyteller said, her voice growing louder with doom.

In the listeners' minds, the trees on the tapa withered and died as life drained from the land, and the island began to turn to dust. Maui somersaulted off a rocky outcropping and raced to the island's edge. High above the ocean, he jumped off a cliff and, in midair, transformed back into a hawk. With a few mighty flaps, he reached his boat.

"Maui tried to escape, but he was confronted by another who sought the heart: Te Kā, a demon of earth and fire!" said the storyteller. Her voice grew deeper and more dramatic. She took a moment to savor making her audience wait.

Te Kā, a massive lava monster, rose up out of ash clouds with great fury, screaming and screeching in anger. Bright volcanic lightning flashed all around, and bits of hot lava spewed from its top as it started toward Maui. Maui brandished his hook and leapt at Te Kā. The two collided, causing a blinding explosion.

"Maui was struck from the sky, never to be seen again. His magical fishhook *and* the heart of

Te Fiti were lost to the sea . . . ," the storyteller said.

The drawing on the tapa showed Maui's hook and Te Fiti's heart as they fell into the rippling ocean waves and disappeared.

Gramma Tala, the storyteller, stood, holding the tapa cloth up for her audience of children to see. Her eyes peeked mysteriously over the tapa, and as she continued with the tale, her voice got louder and louder, building to the finish.

". . . where, even now, a thousand years later, Te Kā and the demons of the deep still lurk, hiding in a darkness that will continue to spread, chasing away our fish, draining the life from island after island, until every one of us is devoured by the bloodthirsty jaws of inescapable death!"

Silence fell as most of Gramma Tala's toddler audience looked up at her with tears in their eyes, terrified. A small boy in the front row sighed and fainted, collapsing to the floor! But one of the girls leaned forward, thrilled by the story. She clapped her hands and smiled excitedly, as if begging for more. The little girl's name was Moana.

"But one day, the heart will be found," continued Gramma Tala, "by someone who will journey beyond our reef, find Maui, deliver him across the great ocean to restore Te Fiti's heart . . . and save us all."

Just as Gramma Tala prepared to launch into another story, Chief Tui hurried in. "Whoa, whoa, whoa! Mother, that's enough." He scooped up Moana and gave her a *hongi,* lovingly pressing his nose and forehead against hers.

"No one goes beyond our reef," he said, reminding the children of the island's most important rule. "We are safe here. There is no darkness; there are no monsters—" He accidentally knocked into the side of the fale, a hut with a thatched roof, causing the tapa screens with the images of monsters painted on them to unravel and wave around. The kids shrieked with fear and jumped on Tui, knocking him over.

"Monster! Monster!" they screamed.

"It's the darkness!" shouted one of the many frightened kids.

"This is how it ends!"

"I'm gonna throw up!"

They continued to scream and pile on top of Tui, kneeing him as they panicked.

"No, no! There is no darkness," Tui said as one of the kids kicked him in his side. "As long as we stay within our reef"—another little knee slammed into his gut—"we'll be fine!" Tui grunted, catching his breath and attempting to calm the children down.

"The legends are true; someone will have to go!" shouted Gramma Tala, feeding the frenzy of fear.

"Mother, Motunui is paradise," said Tui, breaking free from the pileup of toddlers. He dusted himself off and finished his thought. "Who would want to go anywhere else?"

Off in the corner of the fale, little Moana stood in front of the tapa with her big eyes fixed on the image of Te Fiti. As the cloth blew in the wind, Moana could see the vast ocean sparkling between the palm trees in the distance.

It seemed that the ocean was calling to her as the waves danced and waved before breaking on the shore. Moana smiled and stared, mesmerized by the beautiful blue water. Then, without anyone noticing because of all the commotion, she quietly slipped out of the fale.

Chapter 2

Moana walked to the beach and waddled around, enjoying the feel of the sand between her toes. She gazed out at the ocean, its playful waves rolling back and forth, breaking farther out in the distance on the reef that surrounded her island of Motunui. Suddenly, she noticed a beautiful conch shell sparkling in the surf. The shell's creamy pink surface formed a perfect spiral, and Moana wanted to pick it up and hold it. But just as she was about to move closer to it, she heard a loud rustling behind her. She turned to see a group of squawking seabirds tormenting a baby turtle. The turtle was trying to make its way to the water, but the hungry birds blocked its path, threatening to strike. The turtle looked frightened, and each time it tried to take a step, one of the birds lunged for it. The turtle retreated and tried to hide inside its shell.

Moana anxiously eyed the big conch shell. She was afraid that the tide would pull it away before she could get to it. Yet she couldn't leave the baby turtle in its predicament. So she picked up a big leafy palm frond and shielded the turtle as she escorted it across the sand. When the birds tried to go around the palm to get to the turtle, Moana didn't flinch. She bravely shooed them away, stomping her foot to scare them off. She stayed close to the little turtle as its protector, helping it carefully make its way to the water. As the turtle swam into the surf, she stood for a moment, swinging her arms at her sides, and watched it with a grin on her face.

Once the turtle disappeared into the ocean, the

water began to mysteriously spiral and bubble. Then it receded, revealing the conch shell, which a wave had indeed taken. Delighted, Moana squatted to pick it up. As she reached for it, another conch shell appeared, deposited by the receding water. The ocean continued to recede, revealing more and more conch shells. Moana collected them all, balancing the tall pile in her small arms.

The ocean swelled and released a slight wave that curled over Moana and hovered directly above her head. It magically stayed there, seeming to say hello. She grinned up at the wave and poked it with her finger, as if popping a bubble. A trickle of water dripped down over her, making her giggle with delight.

The little wave curled over Moana again, this time playing with her hair and tickling her head. Then, with a twist, it gave her a silly hairstyle. Moana laughed again and again as she played with her strange new friend.

Suddenly, the wave fell back and the ocean parted, forming a canyon. A surprised fish flopped around in the sand at Moana's feet and then found its way back to the safety of the water. Spellbound, Moana toddled along the mysterious canyon, trailing her hand against its watery walls.

This path had led Moana deeper into the ocean, where she saw the baby turtle with its mother by its side. She watched as they swam off together. Once they faded into the distance, her eyes were drawn to a shiny object. It drifted closer, and Moana reached into the water and grabbed it.

The object was round and smooth like a stone on one side, but it had an interesting design on the other. With her finger, Moana traced its unique spiral, curiously feeling the edges of the swirling ridge. She knew there was something very special about this stone.

"Moana!" Her father's panicked voice called her name in the distance, snapping her out of the magical moment. The ocean quickly picked her up and whisked her to shore just before Tui arrived though the trees. As he raced over, Moana accidentally dropped the shiny stone. Tui grabbed her before she could see where it went.

"What are you doing?" Tui said, holding her close. "You scared me."

Moana wriggled in his arms, trying to return to the shore. "Wanna go back," she begged.

"No," he said firmly, facing her. "You don't go out there. It's dangerous."

Moana turned around to glance at the ocean, scanning it for the stone, but she didn't see it. The ocean was once again calm as the gentle waves rippled onto the shore. All the magic appeared to be gone.

Tui set her down and held out his hand. "Moana? Come on. Back to the village."

She reluctantly took her father's hand and walked with him. But she kept her eyes firmly on the ocean until it was out of sight.

Sina, Moana's mother, smiled widely as she approached her family, and the three walked together toward the village.

"You are the next great chief of our people," said Tui, looking down at his daughter.

"And you will do wondrous things, my little minnow," added Sina.

"Oh, yes. But you must learn where you're meant to be," said Tui.

Suddenly, Moana turned from her parents and bolted back to the ocean. Sina and Tui exchanged a worried look and quickly caught up to her. They scooped Moana up and carried her the rest of the way to their safe, quiet village.

Chapter 3

As the years passed, Moana's parents taught her to appreciate life on the island of Motunui. She took comfort in traditions. She learned the songs. She knew what a valuable resource the coconut was—from its sweet meat and water, to its fibers, from which they made nets. She even knew how to weave the different kinds of baskets the villagers used in daily life.

Moana knew that the island gave the people of Motunui all they needed. Yet she was still drawn to the sea. Moana often stared out at the crystal blue water, wondering what was beyond the island's reef. She loved watching the fishing boats as they sailed into the lagoon and returned, but her parents would constantly drag her away, back from the water's edge.

Only Gramma Tala understood Moana's fascination. The two spent many hours walking the beach together and would often dance with the waves. Gramma Tala always encouraged Moana to follow her heart and listen to the voice inside. She told Moana that listening to that voice would help her figure out who she truly was.

One day, Tui led sixteen-year-old Moana up a mountain. They walked higher and higher, until they reached the tallest peak of Motunui. At the very top, Tui showed Moana an enormous pile of stones.

"I've wanted to bring you here from the moment you opened your eyes," said Tui. "This is a sacred place. A place of chiefs." Tui stepped toward the stones and put his hand on them. "There will come a time when you embrace what you're meant to do and who you're meant to be, and you will stand on this peak and place a stone on this mountain, like I did, like my father did, and his father, and every chief that has ever been. And on that day, by adding *your* stone, you will lift this whole island higher. You are the future of our people, Moana. And they are not out there." Tui gestured past the reef, to the vast ocean beyond. "They're right here." He put a hand on Moana's shoulder as the two gazed down toward the village. It was in the distance, at the foot of the mountain. "It's time to be who they need you to be."

Moana glanced back at the pile of stones. She reached out and placed her hand on Tui's stone. This was where her stone would go one day. "Do you think I can?" she asked.

Tui gave Moana a *hongi*. "You will be a great chief, Moana of Motunui . . . if you let yourself."

Moana looked up at her father, thinking about

his words and knowing how important it was to him that she follow in his footsteps. She was finally ready. She would take on the responsibility and be the chief her parents wanted her to be.

She turned her head from the ocean and stayed focused on the island, committed to finding happiness right there. Moana assured herself there was no reason to look beyond the island's reef. Everything she needed and everything she loved was right there.

A few days later, wearing her hei headband decorated with flowers, and with her pet pig, Pua, by her side, she joined her parents and headed to the council meeting. On the way, Moana spotted Gramma Tala dancing with the waves on the shore and paused only a moment before continuing to the council fale.

Drummers banged out a rhythm on large drums as the village council convened. Tui, Sina, and Moana took their places while the drums rapidly built to a dramatic finish. Tui lowered his battle-ax, signaling everyone to sit. Before he could open his mouth to begin the meeting, a booming voice filled the fale. "PEOPLE OF MOTUNUI!" the official announcer yelled. "CHIEF TUI!"

"Thank y—" Chief Tui began, but the man cut him off again.

"OF MOTUNUI!"

"Thank you," said Tui as he turned toward the crowd. "One day, Moana will lead our people. I'm proud to say that out in the village today, you'll see just how far she's come." He gazed at his daughter with love and handed her the chief's battle-ax. Moana smiled, feeling his pride. Everyone turned to her, as she now had the floor.

Moana smiled graciously and took a deep breath, but before she could say anything, the loud voice rang out again. "MOANA OF MOTUNUI!" he screamed right into Moana's ear. She accidentally dropped the heavy battle-ax, nearly chopping off Pua's snout!

Throughout the day, Moana was acting Chief of Motunui to the village as her parents observed her making rounds across the island.

When a villager named Maivia complained about his leaky roof, Moana climbed up to the rafters to check it out. Maivia explained to Tui and Sina, "Every storm, the roof leaks on the fire, no matter how many fronds I add—"

From the top of the fale, Moana yelled, "Fixed!" She smiled down at them. "It wasn't the fronds; the wind shifted the supports," she said. Then she took a bite of food that Maivia offered her. "*That's good pork.*" She saw Pua by her feet and suddenly felt very bad for sharing that so loudly.

Later, Moana stood beside a large man named Tolo, holding his hand as he got a new tattoo on his back.

"Ow. Ow. Ow," repeated Tolo over and over again, gripping Moana's hand tighter and tighter.

"You're doing great," said Moana, trying to sound normal as she attempted to withstand the pain of his strong squeezes.

Hours later, Moana continued to hold Tolo's hand even as she felt her hand going numb. "Just five more hours," she said to Tolo, wincing in pain.

He squeezed her hand a bit harder. "Ow. Ow. Ow . . ."

When Tolo's tattoo was finally complete, he stood up and gave Moana a hug, thanking her for her support. Then he hobbled off, walking stiffly toward his fale as Moana tried to shake the soreness out of her hand.

Tolo's friend Asoleilei walked by with a big energetic smile and congratulated him. *"Manuia!"* he shouted, slapping him on the rear. That caused Tolo to wince from the pain, and quickly move away from his friend.

Pua tried to keep up as Moana continued the village rounds, helping anyone who needed it. Two little girls and a little boy ran up to her, out of breath, and launched into a story. They spoke loud and fast, talking over each other, as they tried to explain.

"Lua hit me," said Loa.

"And Loa hit me back," said Lua.

"But Loa was like, *Wawomodo?*" said Loa.

"'What would Moana do?'" explained La'a.

"Which is just be awesome," said Lua.

"So she stopped punching my face," said Loa.

"And made you a picture," said La'a.

The kids held up a terrible drawing of Moana stopping a fierce, bloody fight. Moana stared at it, trying to decide how to react.

"That's blood," Lua pointed out.

Moana smiled and took the drawing, thanking each of them for the special gift.

Later, a village cook named Vela found Moana and approached her with a question.

"I was wondering about the chicken there eating the rock," Vela said. She gestured to Heihei, a wacky-looking rooster with expressionless, crooked eyes who was trying to swallow a stone. "He seems to lack the minimum intelligence required for self-preservation. Would it be more humane to just cook him?"

Moana watched as Heihei coughed up the stone and then went back to pecking at it. "Well, sometimes our strengths lie beneath the surface," she said. "Far beneath, in some cases. But I'm sure there's more to Heihei than meets the eye."

As Moana continued on her rounds, she met a troubled farmer who showed her the latest crop of coconuts.

"It's the harvest," the farmer said. "This morning, I was cleaning the coconuts, and . . ." Moana cracked open a seemingly healthy coconut, revealing its black, rotten insides. She leaned in to take a closer look. Tui and Sina peered over Moana to get a glimpse of the terrible sight. Everyone looked at her, waiting to see what she would say.

"Well, um . . . we should clear the diseased trees. And move to a new grove." Moana pointed to an unclaimed area of land and said, "There."

The farmer nodded in agreement, and Tui and Sina exchanged a proud look.

Feeling great, Moana turned toward her loving parents and the majestic mountain behind them. Then she looked out to the blue ocean, deep in thought. She loved her family, her island, and her village. And she wanted to do what was right for everyone. Finally, she glanced at her father with a sly smile.

"I was thinking I might skip dinner," she said.

"Is everything all right?" asked Tui, concerned.

"Mmm-hmm. I'd rather just take a walk . . . up the mountain," Moana said, her smile widening.

It took a moment for Tui to understand what she was really saying. Finally, he grinned and stumbled over his words, too proud and happy to speak clearly. "You . . . Yes, if . . . So you . . . ," Tui said to Sina. "She's . . . Moana wants to take a walk up the mountain." He lowered his head and quietly added, "She means her stone."

Sina smiled, amused. "I got that."

As they headed to their fale, a fisherman named Lasalo hurried over to them. "Am I too late?" he asked.

Tui stepped up to the man. "Actually, Moana needs to—"

"How can I help?" asked Moana, facing the fisherman.

Lasalo somberly led Moana to the beach, with

Tui and Sina behind them. They stood next to the fishing boat as the fisherman lifted out a net and showed it to Moana. It was completely empty.

"Our nets in the east lagoon are pulling up less and less," Lasalo said.

"Well, then we'll rotate the fishing grounds," said Moana.

"We'll rotate the fishing grounds," Tui repeated.

Anxious to get Moana up to Motunui's tallest peak, Tui tried to usher her away. But Lasalo continued. "Uh, we have no fish," he said.

"Oh, then we'll fish the far side of the island," offered Moana, gesturing toward it.

"We tried," said Lasalo.

"The windward side?" she asked, her concern growing.

"And the leeward side, the shallows, the channel; we've tried the whole lagoon! They're just gone," Lasalo said.

Moana's face fell as she stared down the beach at the other fishing boats, all returning with empty nets. It wasn't too long ago that she'd watch the boats come in hauling nets bursting with fish. She wondered, *How could they all be gone?*

"I will talk to the council," said Tui. "I'm sure we can find a solution."

Moana looked toward the lagoon and her eyes moved beyond the reef to the open ocean; it was new territory. The fishermen had not cast their nets there. She climbed up on a boat to get a better view and took in the vastness of the sea. It was the obvious choice.

"What if . . . we fish beyond the reef?" Moana asked.

The fishermen seemed surprised. Tui and Sina were completely shocked.

"No one goes beyond the reef," Tui said, trying to stay calm.

"I know, but if we have no fish in the lagoon—"

"Moana—"

"And there's a whole ocean—"

Tui tried to reach for her, but Moana stepped to the front of the boat.

"We have one rule," Tui said, raising his voice.

"An old rule, when there were fish—"

"A rule that keeps us safe instead of endangering our people!" yelled Tui.

Moana stared at her father, feeling both angry and ashamed of his outburst.

Tui was furious. He knew in his heart that Moana would always yearn to sail the open ocean, and he felt that she was selfishly looking for an excuse to do just that. He gritted his teeth, watching Moana standing steadfast on the boat, and then he pulled her back to the sand.

"Every time I think you're past this . . . ," Tui said. Then he walked away. "No one goes beyond the reef!" he shouted as he picked up his pace, fuming.

Chapter 4

On the shore, Moana grunted as she angrily hurled a coconut to the ground in an attempt to vent her frustrations. She picked up one after another. She hit them with an oar, trying to drive them into the sand, even as her mother approached.

"At least you didn't say it in front of everybody, standing on a boat," said Sina, trying to lighten the mood.

Moana whacked another coconut.

"I didn't say 'fish beyond the reef' because I want to be on the ocean."

"But you still do," said Sina gently. She glanced down at Moana's hand tightly gripping the oar and sighed.

Unable to deny it, Moana turned away. It was true; she still heard the ocean's call and longed to explore it.

Sina continued. "He's hard on you because—"

"Because he doesn't get me," Moana said.

"Because he *was* you," Sina corrected her. "Drawn to the water, he took a boat, Moana. He crossed the reef and found an unforgiving sea. Waves like mountains. His best friend begged to be out on that boat. Your father couldn't save him." Sina's voice trailed off; the memory was too sad to relive. She looked lovingly at Moana. "He's hoping he can save you."

Moana's anger turned to sadness and guilt. In the village, she could see Tui dealing with the panicked villagers. She knew how much her father loved the people of Motunui and how heavy the responsibility of protecting them lay upon his shoulders. She felt terrible.

Moana wished her father understood that she loved the people, too. That was why she wanted to go beyond the reef—to find fish. So that everyone would have plenty to eat.

"Sometimes, who we wish we were, what we wish we could do . . . it's just not meant to be." Sina took the oar from Moana and put it on the ground.

"If you were me, what would you do?" asked Moana.

Sina brushed the hair away from Moana's face. "We must make our own choices, my little minnow," she said. "No matter how hard they may be." She left Moana alone to think about what she had said.

Moana focused on the horizon. In her imagination, the sea seemed endless and full of possibility. With thoughts flooding her mind, she walked up to the highest peak on Motunui. At the top, she held a stone in her hand, trying to sort out her feelings.

She wanted to make her parents and her village proud. She wanted to do what was right. But how could she quiet the voice inside her? She couldn't help her curiosity about the ocean. She wondered how far the sea went and what was out there. She also wondered why the voice inside her seemed so different from everybody else's. And how would she ever make peace with her father's wishes for her future?

The sun's reflection off the ocean sparkled in her eyes as the water called to her. No matter how much she wanted to, she couldn't ignore it. She couldn't pretend to be someone she wasn't. She dropped the stone and ran down to the shore.

Pua picked up the oar in his mouth and offered it to her before he hopped on a small boat as Moana pushed it into the water. The boat wobbled a bit as Moana found her balance, and Pua seemed more than a little nervous.

"We're okay, Pua," said Moana, trying to find her confidence. "There's more fish beyond the reef. There's more beyond the reef."

She paddled out into the water, feeling a rush of excitement as a wave carried her high on its crest. But then the wind changed and the boom swung toward her! It just missed her head. But as Moana breathed a sigh of relief, a massive wave rushed toward her, breaking before she could react. It slammed into the boat and knocked Pua overboard! The little pig flailed around, struggling to stay afloat.

"Pua!" Moana yelled, trying to get to him. But an even bigger wave crashed down, knocking her into the sea as well. She surfaced with Pua in her arms and shoved him onto the broken outrigger. A moment later, rough waves caused the boat to slam into her head and push her underwater.

Her foot was wedged into a cluster of coral on the ocean floor, trapping Moana underwater. She strained as she tried to swim upward, but she was unable to wriggle free.

Spotting a rock, she grabbed it and smashed the coral, releasing her foot. Using all her might, she pushed off the ocean floor and shot up, gasping for air.

The waves finally pushed Moana and Pua up

onto Motunui's sandy shore. Completely unaffected by the ordeal, Pua gave Moana a cheerful lick and ran off to chase birds. Moana breathed heavily, happy to fill her lungs with air as she collected herself. She looked down at her foot, scraped and bleeding from the sharp coral. The boat she had borrowed was smashed to pieces, which floated in the water and washed up onto the sand. She knew she would be in big trouble for what she had done.

"Whatever just happened . . . blame it on the pig," said a familiar voice.

Moana turned to see Gramma Tala emerging from behind some flowering shrubs.

"Gramma?" Moana asked, moving her foot behind her as she tried to hide it. But Gramma Tala placed her walking stick behind Moana's ankle and used it to pick up her leg, getting a closer look at the wound. "Are you gonna tell Dad?" Moana asked.

"If you lost a toe, maybe," Gramma Tala said.

More pieces of the broken boat washed up beside them. Moana shook her head. "He was right about going out there," she said. She felt a momentary sense of relief. "It's time. I'm putting my stone on the mountain."

Gramma Tala studied Moana's face for a moment. Then she looked back at the ocean and breathed in the salty air. Suddenly, a school of elegant manta rays swam up, gracefully flapping their fins.

Gramma Tala pushed past Moana to get closer to them as they slid through the water. Moana could see the big manta ray tattoo stretched across her grandmother's back as she watched the animals.

"Well, okay then," Gramma Tala said. "Head on back; put that stone up there."

Moana started to walk away. But she turned back to Gramma Tala after taking only a few steps. "Why aren't you trying to talk me out of it?" she asked.

"Because you said that's what you wanted," said Gramma Tala.

"It is," said Moana.

Gramma Tala nodded without saying a word.

Moana headed back toward the village. But just as she was about to cross the flowering shrubs that lined the beach, Gramma Tala spoke up. "When I die, I'm going to come back as one of these," she said, gesturing to the manta rays as they continued to swim, swirling in front of her in a circle. Her tattoo wiggled between her shoulders as she danced, swinging her hips and moving her arms in time with the waves striking the shore. "Or I chose the wrong tattoo." She looked back at Moana with a smirk.

"Why are you acting weird?" asked Moana.

"I'm the village crazy lady . . . that's my job," Gramma Tala replied.

"If there's something you want to tell me, just tell me," said Moana. She sounded almost desperate for her grandmother's advice. It would be nice to hear someone say she *should* listen to the call of the ocean. "Is there something you want to tell me?"

Gramma Tala leaned in and whispered, "Is there something you want to hear?" Then she smiled mysteriously and hobbled off, using her walking stick to help her over the rough terrain. Moana followed right behind, and she couldn't help but smile, too. She didn't know where Gramma Tala was going, but wherever it was, it would be an adventure. And it would involve a story.

Chapter 5

At the very edge of the island, the moon glowed high above. Gramma Tala carried a torch and climbed a steep path, with Moana following. It was a treacherous path of jagged lava rocks along dark crashing waves that erupted in sprays of sea foam. Gramma Tala stopped for a moment to catch her breath before continuing. Moana tried to help her, but Gramma Tala shooed her away, determined to do it on her own.

"You've been told all our people's stories . . . but one," said Gramma Tala, continuing the climb.

She held up her walking stick and used it to move aside a tangle of overgrown vines. Behind them were large stones that blocked a hidden lava tube. Gramma Tala used her stick to try to loosen one of the stones, but it wouldn't budge.

"What is this place?" asked Moana, helping to move the rock.

"You really think our ancestors stayed within the reef?" Gramma Tala asked, her eyes flashing in the dancing light of the torch.

Moana knocked down the rest of the rocks, revealing a large opening. A gust of wind whipped through the cavern, blowing her hair from her face and sending a chill that tingled through her body.

"Ooooooh," Gramma Tala said with an air of mystery.

"What's in there?" Moana asked, her curiosity growing by the second.

"The answer."

"To what?"

"The question you keep asking yourself. Who are you meant to be?" Gramma Tala handed her the torch. "Go inside . . . bang the drum . . . and find out."

Moana stared into the darkness for a moment before slowly climbing through the hole and into the dark lava tube.

Carefully placing one foot in front of the other, she walked past dripping walls. As she moved deeper, a low rumbling sound began to build, and soon she could tell it was the sound of a waterfall. Intrigued, she picked up her pace. When she stepped around an enormous boulder, she saw something that nearly knocked her to her knees—a giant hidden cavern filled with dozens of ocean-voyaging boats!

She rushed toward the boats in awe and ran her hand along their smooth wooden sides, looking up at the majestic sails towering above. She jumped from boat to boat, exploring them, amazed by their beauty and intrigued by the adventures they must have seen.

The wide waterfall poured into the cavern's glistening pool. It also helped disguise the entrance from the sea so that it could not be seen from the outside. A canoe floated at the foot of the waterfall. Excited, Moana jumped onto the hull and maneuvered the boom. As the sail swung around, it revealed a massive double-hulled canoe behind it. Each hull was a support float that helped the boat stay steady on the ocean. Moana knew by looking at it, that the canoe had carried many things.

Moana climbed onto the double-hulled canoe's upper deck and noticed a log drum. "Bang the drum," she said to herself, repeating her grandmother's words.

Moana picked up a thick pair of wooden sticks that sat beside the drum and tentatively banged on it. Nothing happened. She banged again, this time a bit louder, and waited, wondering if something was going to happen. It was quiet for another moment, but then suddenly she heard an echo—a rhythm as clear as an old, familiar song.

Moana listened carefully, then banged out the same rhythm, and something did happen. *Whoosh!*

The chilly wind returned, and lines of torches magically lit, illuminating the tapa sail of the boat.

Moana stared at the sail as it filled with wind and began to move, rhythmically waving. The drum continued to play, banging out an ancient pattern that reverberated against the stone cavern walls, filling it with music.

In Moana's imagination, a shadowy sea came to life on the sail, as if it were right in front of her. It played out the story of her ancestors: voyagers who navigated the ocean by the wind, the moon, and the stars at night. They used the sun, waves, and currents to find their way during the day. Captivated, Moana watched as the sail showed how the adventurous group voyaged from island to island over the rolling swells of the ocean, unafraid of its endlessness, unafraid of the far-off horizon line. They were confident and proud. And when it was time to find a new home, they bravely sailed across the ocean to find one.

"We were voyagers," Moana said, letting the surprising fact sink into her mind. "We were voyagers!" she repeated. She could hardly contain her excitement.

Outside the secret cavern, Gramma Tala could hear Moana as she raced back out yelling, "WE WERE VOYAGERS!" Shaking, she sat down next to Gramma Tala on a rock and asked, "Why'd we stop?"

Gramma Tala grunted and said one word: "Maui." She pointed to the horizon, and Moana pictured it coming to life in her mind, seeing images to match Gramma Tala's tale. "When he stole from the mother island, darkness fell, Te Kā awoke, monsters lurked, and boats stopped coming back. To protect our people, the ancient chiefs forbade voyaging and we forgot who we were." She looked up at the island. "And the darkness has continued to spread, chasing out fish, draining the life from island after island."

Snapping out of the story, Gramma Tala motioned to the bluff. It was turning black! Moana touched a darkened vine, and it crumbled in her hand, leaving nothing but a pile of dust.

"Our island!" Moana said, concerned.

"But one day, someone will journey beyond our reef, find Maui, deliver him across the great ocean to restore the heart of Te Fiti . . . ," said Gramma Tala.

Gramma Tala placed a special stone in Moana's hand. Moana gazed at its spiral and suddenly remembered finding it all those years ago after the conch shell. ". . . and save us all," Moana said, mesmerized.

Gramma Tala smiled. "I was there," she said. "The ocean chose you."

"I—I thought it was a dream," said Moana, tracing the stone's deep-ridged spiral. It was the heart of Te Fiti.

As she continued to drag her finger, the water whirled faster and faster around them, forming a circle in the shallows, with Moana at its center. The majestic whirlpool rose around them, exhibiting its strength and power.

"Nope," Gramma Tala said, assuring Moana it had not been a dream. Then she pointed her walking stick at the sky, showing Moana a hook constellation. "Our ancestors believed Maui lies at the bottom of his hook. Follow it; you will find him."

Moana stared at the heart in her hand. "But . . . why would it choose *me*?" she asked. "I don't even know how to get past the reef." She thought for a moment and suddenly said, "But I know who does!"

Moana got up and ran toward the village as fast as she could.

Gramma Tala watched Moana go and sat back down, exhaling.

Chapter 6

While Tui led the village council, people complained about the poor harvest and the lack of fish. A worried chatter filled the fale. "More crops are turning black," said one villager.

"We won't have enough food," said another.

"It's happening all over the island," said another.

The troubled sounds of the villagers began to build as the comments intensified and people all started talking at once.

Trying his best to calm them and regain order, Tui said, "Then we will dig new fields; we will—"

Suddenly, Moana burst in. "We can stop the darkness and save our island!" she shouted. "The heart of Te Fiti is real."

Everyone stopped talking, and an awkward silence fell. They all stared at Moana as if she were crazy.

"There's a cavern of boats, huge canoes. . . . We can take them, find Maui, make him restore the heart," Moana continued, exhilarated. She held the heart up to Tui. "We were voyagers; we can voyage again."

The villagers looked to Tui, confused and anxiously waiting for his response. Without a word, he pulled Moana out of the fale.

"You told me to help our people. *This* is how we help our people!" Moana said.

Tui walked past her, grabbing a torch. "I should've burned those boats a long time ago."

"What? *No!*" Moana said, pulling on Tui's arm. "We have to find Maui. We have to restore the heart!"

Tui grabbed the heart out of her hand. "There is no heart! This is just a rock!" he shouted, throwing it into the bushes.

"No!" Moana scrambled around, searching for the heart. She found it in the tall grass and clutched it in her hand, but then something else on the ground caught her eye: Gramma Tala's walking stick. Moana picked it up, concerned. "Gramma . . ."

The blare of a conch shell wailed in the distance as a warrior raced up wearing a grave expression. "Chief," he said. "Your mother!"

Moana ran toward Gramma Tala's fale as fast as she could. She made her way through a group of villagers who circled the outside of the hut. Inside, Moana found Gramma Tala on her back, almost lifeless. Sina sat by her side. Tui rushed in, and he and Moana shared a worried look.

"We found her at the edge of the water," said the warrior.

"What can be done?" asked Tui.

Moana watched him talk to the warrior, slowly moving closer to listen in on their conversation, when she felt a hand gently touch hers. She turned to see Gramma Tala reaching out to her and trying to whisper something.

Moana bent down close, putting her ear next to Gramma Tala's lips.

"Go," Gramma Tala whispered.

"Not now, I can't," said Moana.

"You must." Gramma Tala's voice sounded weak and raspy. "The ocean chose you. Follow the fishhook—"

"Gramma—"

"And when you find Maui, you grab him by the ear, and you say, 'I am Moana of Motunui. . . . You will board my boat, sail across the sea, and restore the heart of Te Fiti.'"

"I can't leave you," said Moana with tears in her eyes.

"There is nowhere you could go that I won't be with you. You will find a way, Moana," Gramma Tala said, giving her a *hongi*. "You will find your way. . . ."

As the healer hurried in, Gramma Tala pressed her shell necklace into Moana's hand and whispered, "Go."

Moana glanced down at the necklace. She remembered seeing the first ancestor with the same sunrise shell necklace in the wayfinders' cavern. He had placed it around the neck of the young wayfinder, someone who used the sun, wind, moon, stars, and currents to navigate with, who sailed off in search of new islands.

She wrapped her hand tightly around it and backed out of the fale. Outside, she looked up at the stars twinkling against the dark night sky and scanned them, searching for the constellation of Maui's hook. She found it, and without another thought, Moana placed Te Fiti's heart securely inside Gramma Tala's necklace and fastened it around her neck. She had made up her mind. She was going to go.

Moana hurried to her fale and collected supplies. Sina appeared and surprised Moana by handing her a rope, along with a few more things for her journey. They stared at each other, trying to read each other's thoughts. Then Sina moved aside, allowing Moana to walk by.

Moana hurried out of the village, passing a black banyan tree, its dead leaves crunching beneath her feet. She went to the secret cavern and climbed into one of the canoes.

Pushing off, she launched the boat and paddled through the great waterfall into the lagoon.

As she sailed out, she turned back toward her village and saw the light in Gramma Tala's fale go out. Moana knew that meant Gramma had passed away, and she felt a great sadness. Suddenly, a glow appeared on the shore, catching her eye. It streaked through the water toward her. As it rocketed under the boat, she could see that it was a spectral manta ray. It continued toward the open ocean, breaching over the reef, illuminating a safe passage for Moana to follow.

With the light of the moon above and the manta ray below, Moana felt certain she was doing the right thing.

Determined, she paddled toward the reef, and as a wave swelled toward her, she opened her sail, ready to face it. She guided the canoe over the massive swell, riding the wave, and as it crashed, Moana blasted over the reef!

She looked back once more at the island of Motunui and watched as her home disappeared in the distance. Turning her eyes to the open ocean, Moana felt a rush of excitement.

She gazed up at the stars and focused on the constellation of Maui's hook. With her fingers curled around the necklace, she set out to find the demigod.

Chapter 7

Moana paddled through the night and into the next day. With the bright sun shining down, she repeated and rehearsed what Gramma Tala had told her to say to Maui, like a mantra. "I am Moana of Motunui, you will board my boat, sail across the sea, and restore the heart of Te Fiti. I am Moana of—" A strange clucking noise stopped her, and she peered into the cargo hold of the boat.

A coconut rose up, and the sound was loud and clear: *Bagock!*

"Heihei?" Moana said, removing the coconut

to reveal the silly rooster. Heihei took one look at the ocean and his crooked eyes went wide. He screeched and screamed as if attempting to seek help from every corner of the ocean! Moana quickly placed the coconut back over his head to silence him. She removed it, and he screeched again. She placed it back on, and he was quiet. She pulled it off once more, and he did not react at all.

"It's okay, see?" said Moana. "You're all right. There we go, yeah, nice water. The ocean's a friend of mine." Heihei looked at the water and walked right off the boat! His scrawny clawed feet stuck straight up as he bobbed up and down in the sea.

Moana jumped in to save him, and the boat started moving away from her. Holding on to Heihei, she swam for the boat, grabbing it before it drifted too far. Once they were back on board, Heihei tried to walk off again, so Moana put him in the cargo hold and told him to stay there.

"Okay, next stop: Maui," Moana said, grabbing the oar. Then she returned to practicing her speech, figuring out exactly how to say it and which words to emphasize. "I am Moana of Motunui. You will board my boat, sail across the sea, and restore the heart of Te Fiti."

Later that night, Moana struggled, trying to keep the boat on course through strong winds. "I am Moana of Motunui," she chanted. "You will board my boat, sail across the sea, and restore the heart of Te Fiti."

It wasn't long before she became very tired, but she continued repeating her speech. "I . . . am Moana . . . of . . . Motu . . . ," she said, slurring her words. The ocean splashed her awake. "Board my boat!" she shouted, but when she looked up for the constellation, she couldn't find it. She spun around and there it was, behind her! As she tried to change directions, the wind pushed her off balance and the boat started to tip. She tried to right it, but the boat capsized, sending her into the ocean. She rose to the surface to see her food floating away—along with her oar. She decided to splash the water, trying to get its attention. "Uh, ocean . . . can I get a little help?" she asked.

While she waited for the ocean to respond, she tried to collect her things. Then a deep rumbling noise thundered from the sky. A storm was brewing. Giving up on her supplies, she reached for her oar and tried to right the boat.

"Come on. . . . Help! *Come on!*" she begged the ocean. "Help me! PLEASE!"

But the waves grew bigger and became more violent. Moana helplessly clung to the canoe as it was tossed around the rough sea like a tiny toy boat. A mountainous wave came toward her and crashed down hard. Then everything went black.

When Moana opened her eyes, she found herself washed up on an island. She spit the sand from her mouth and shook herself off. Her canoe was on its side, and Heihei was standing on the mast, with a basket on his head. He stepped off, falling to the ground, his head buried in the sand and his clawed feet sticking straight up. Moana immediately felt her necklace. She was relieved to find the heart of Te Fiti still safe inside.

Moana studied her boat and then walked angrily to the water's edge. "Um . . . what? I said 'help me,' and tidal-waving my boat? NOT HELPING!" she shouted, kicking her foot toward the ocean. The water retreated, causing her to fall on her rear. She took another look at her boat and then turned back to the ocean.

"Fish pee in you! All day! So . . . ," Moana said, pointing to the ocean. It made her feel just a tiny bit better.

Heihei, with his head still stuck in the basket, pecked at a big rock. But this wasn't a regular rock. It was covered in thousands of check marks that together formed the shape of a giant fishhook! She scanned the ground and spotted oversized footprints that led to a makeshift camp.

"Maui . . . ?" Moana said.

An ocean wave gestured toward her, giving what looked like a very human nod.

She lowered her eyes sheepishly, realizing the

ocean *had* helped get her there. But before she could apologize, she heard a noise and a giant shadow approached. Moana gasped.

"Maui," she said nervously.

Chapter 8

Moana clutched her oar in one hand and Heihei in the other as she ducked behind the boat, trying to prepare herself. "Maui, demigod of the wind and sea? I am Moana of Motunui. You will board my boat—no—you *will* board my boat—you will *board* my *boat*, yeah."

"Boat!" a deep voice rumbled all around her. "A BOAT!"

A man suddenly appeared, but he was more like a mountain! His dark, muscular body was covered in a tapestry of tattoos, and a wild, curly mop of black hair fell around his broad shoulders. A necklace of whale teeth hung around his neck, and he wore a skirt made of big green banana leaves. The man smiled from ear to ear, revealing a slight gap in his two front teeth, as he joyfully lifted the boat. "THE GODS HAVE GIVEN ME A B— *AGH!*" He was so shocked to see Moana that he almost dropped the boat on her head. He lifted it again but only saw Heihei, buried in the sand up to his neck. Confused, he looked around.

Moana popped up behind him. "Maui?"

As he turned to face Moana, the boat he was still holding almost knocked her down.

Moana recovered, and as Maui loomed over her, she forced the words to come out of her mouth. "Shape-shifter? Demigod of the wind and sea?" Moana tried her best to sound confident. She took a deep breath. "I am Moan—"

"Hero of men," Maui said, interrupting her.

"What?"

"Maui, shape-shifter, demigod of the wind and sea, hero of men. I interrupted. From the top—

hero of men. Go," Maui instructed her.

"Uh—I am Mo—" Moana started.

"Sorry, sorry, and women. Men *and* women—both, all—not a guy/girl thing—hero to all," Maui said. "You're doing great," he added in a whisper.

Confused, Moana pushed her oar toward him. "What—no, I'm here to—" Moana started.

"Of course, yes, Maui always has time for his fans," said Maui, assuming she was just too taken with his charm and beauty to speak coherently. He grabbed the oar from her and picked up Heihei, gripping him like a pen. Then he used Heihei's beak to scratch the symbol of a hook onto the oar, signing his autograph. He added a heart. He winked at her as he finished signing with a dramatic flair. "Eh? I know, not every day you meet your hero—"

Moana looked down at the autograph and then jabbed Maui in the gut with the oar. He doubled over, and she grabbed his ear.

"You are not my hero! You are the dirt basket who stole the heart of Te Fiti!" she yelled, showing

MOANA is the daughter of Chief Tui of Motunui. She is a strong and caring sixteen-year-old who wants to explore the ocean against her father's wishes.

HEIHEI is the slow-witted village rooster that accidentally stows away on Moana's seafaring quest. Maui nicknames him Drumstick.

PUA is Moana's pet pig. When Moana leaves Motunui, he waits patiently for her return, and he is glad to greet her when she comes back.

MAUI is a demigod—half god, half mortal, all awesome. Charismatic and funny, he wields a magical fishhook that allows him to shape-shift into all kinds of animals and pull up islands from the sea.

Moana and Maui form an uneasy alliance. They encounter bandits called the KAKAMORA, the crab monster TAMATOA, and the lava monster TE KĀ on their many adventures.

Moana helps Maui sharpen his **SHAPE-SHIFTING** skills after he loses his confidence, and Maui teaches Moana how to **WAYFIND**.

Maui teaches Moana, Pua, and Heihei
how to make **WARRIOR FACES**.

Moana and Maui eventually sail to the island of TE FITI despite the dangers they know they will face.

him the heart. "And you *will* board my boat, sail across the sea, and put it back!" She tried to pull Maui toward the boat, but it was like trying to move a brick wall. He wouldn't budge. Maui placed his giant hand on top of Moana's head and pulled her off the ground with ease. He set her down on the sand and looked at her, a bit confused.

"Um, yeah . . . almost sounded like you don't like me, which is impossible, 'cause everyone knows I only got stuck here trying to get the heart for you mortals. . . . But what I believe you were trying to say . . . is thank you," said Maui.

"Thank you?" Moana was stunned.

"You're welcome," replied Maui.

"What? No, that's not—I wasn't—" said Moana, sputtering to try to explain.

Once again, Maui interrupted her and started talking more specifically about how great he was.

Maui pointed out one of his tattoos, showing it to Moana. It was a small image of himself—a Mini Maui. The tattoo came to life and gave Maui a high five. Then Mini Maui hopped across Maui's body, from tattoo to tattoo, as Maui told Moana about all the wonderful things he had done for the world.

Moana watched, amazed, as the animated tattoos played out the stories of Maui's great accomplishments. One tattoo showed how Maui stole fire from the fierce earthquake god to bring it to the humans. Another showed him lassoing the sun to stretch out the daylight hours. With Mini Maui acting as guide, the tattoos continued to illustrate how Maui had helped humankind with just about everything: the sky, the tides, the breeze, the grass—even the coconut trees!

Once he had finished describing his glorious past, Maui smiled and said one final "You're welcome." Then he swiftly shoved Moana into a cave, rolled a boulder over the entrance, and trapped her inside! "Thank you," he added. Moana yelled, but Maui simply skipped down to the beach, excited to get into Moana's canoe and finally leave the island.

Mini Maui pulled at Maui's arm angrily. "What?" said Maui, looking at the tattoo. "No, I'm not going to Te Fiti with some kid; I'm gonna go get my hook. You have yours; I need mine." Maui put a finger on the tattoo. "Talk to the back," he said, flicking it over his shoulder and onto his back.

Bagock! clucked Heihei.

Maui grabbed Heihei by the neck and smiled as he eyed the rooster. "Boat snack!" he said. Then he hauled the canoe into the water and climbed on board.

Inside Maui's cave, Moana threw her body against the boulder, but it was far too big and heavy for her to move. She looked around, searching for another way out, and sprinted into a narrow canyon. It dead-ended at a platform where Maui had been sculpting a life-sized statue of himself. Moana scanned the area, looking for options. It seemed as though the only way out was up through the steep funnel cliff. But how could she get to it?

She climbed the statue of Maui, which was so tall it reached the top of the cave. Then she pressed her feet against the side of the cave, using all her strength to push the statue over on its side. She jumped on top of it and rode it as it tumbled toward the opening. Once she was directly underneath the funnel, she leapt up and wedged her body into the opening. With her hands and feet flat against the narrow walls, she climbed toward the blue sky.

Meanwhile, Maui danced on the deck of the boat. "Goodbye, island!" he sang. Mini Maui nudged him. "Don't look at me like that. It's a beautiful cave; she's gonna love it," he said. Then he looked at Heihei. "And I'm gonna love you. In my belly. Let's fatten you up, Drumstick," he said, sprinkling food for the rooster.

Heihei pecked around but kept missing the bits of food.

Moana made it all the way to the top of the funnel cliff. When she reached the opening, she thrust her body out, feet first. From the cliff, she spotted Maui in the ocean below and sprinted ahead. Then she yelled like a warrior and fearlessly jumped off the rocky overhang toward him. But Moana fell short and belly-flopped into the water.

"I could watch that all day," Maui said. "Okay,

enjoy the island. Maui out!" Maui trimmed the sail, or moved the sails so they got the most wind, and took off, leaving Moana in his wake.

Moana swam after him but was not getting any closer to the boat. "No!" she yelled. "Stop! HEY! You have to put back the heart—stop! Maui! MAUI!"

Just then, the ocean sucked Moana underwater and dragged her toward Maui at turbo speed. It carried her all the way to the boat, lifted her up, and dumped her on board. She stood there dripping wet as she and Maui stared at each other, shocked.

"Did not see that coming," said Maui.

Moana boldly faced Maui and started her speech. "I am Moana of Motunui. This is my canoe, and you *will* journey to Te Fiti—"

Moana screeched as Maui picked her up and tossed her overboard. Mini Maui popped back up, mad at him. "Get over it," Maui said to the tattoo figure. "We've gotta move."

But before Maui could start sailing—*floomp!*—the ocean tossed Moana back onto the front of the boat.

"And she's back," said Maui.

"I am Moana of Motunuiiii—"

Maui dug the oar into the water, putting on the brakes, which caused Moana to fall off again. In a flash, the ocean put her right back onto the boat.

"It was Moana, right?" said Maui, wearing a deadpan expression.

"Yes, and you will restore the heart—" she said, holding the heart out to Maui. He grabbed it and threw it a mile out to sea.

Whack! The ocean threw it right back, knocking Maui in the head. He looked at Moana. "Okay, I'm out," he said, diving over the side.

But just as he hit the water, the sea threw him back onto the boat. "OH, COME ON!" he shouted. The ocean splashed him in the face.

"What is your problem?" said Moana. "Are . . . you afraid of it?" She held the heart closer to Maui, and he backed up.

"No," Maui said, chuckling nervously. "No, I'm not afraid."

Mini Maui disagreed, nodding and nervously biting his fingernails to show Moana the truth:

Maui was definitely afraid of the heart.

Maui scowled at the tattoo. "Stay out of it, or I will put you on my butt," he said. Then he turned to Moana. "Stop it. That's not a heart; it's a curse. Second I took it, I got blasted outta the sky and lost my hook. Get it away."

"Get *this* away?" Moana said, taunting him, inching the heart closer and closer. She was thoroughly enjoying seeing him squirm. "I am a demigod; I will smite you," said Maui, dodging her. "You wanna get smote? Smoten? *Agh!* Listen to me—that thing doesn't create life; it's a homing beacon of death. You don't put it away, bad things will come for it!"

"Come for *this*? The heart? You mean THIS HEART RIGHT HERE?"

Maui was getting worried and stammered as she waved it around his face. "Hey—will ya—cut it—" Fed up, he faced Moana and firmly said, "You're gonna get us killed."

"No, I'm gonna get us to Te Fiti so you can put it back. Thank you," said Moana. Then, deepening her voice to mimic Maui, she said, "You're welcome."

Thunk! A huge spear soared through the air and sank into the side of their boat, barely missing Heihei. The clueless rooster started pecking at it. Moana and Maui looked around to see where the spear had come from. Through the fog, they could barely make out a large silhouette. . . . Whatever it was, it was getting closer.

Chapter 9

"**K**akamora," sighed Maui.

"Kaka—what?" asked Moana.

"Kaka*mora*. Murdering little pirates. Wonder what they're here for," he said sarcastically, giving Moana an irritated look.

As the Kakamora approached, Moana saw a strange-looking, island-sized vessel. A little warrior in coconut armor stood on top of it, and then two more warriors ran up to join him. They knocked on their shells with their knuckles, communicating with each other in snappy little beats.

"They're . . . kinda . . . cute?" said Moana, confused.

The coconut warriors used their fingers to paint red angry faces on their shells, and big bass drums sounded as their chief beat out a thunderous rhythm. The chief aimed a battle-ax at the heart of Te Fiti in Moana's hand, and the Kakamora immediately started loading dozens of spears into their catapults.

"What do we do?" Moana asked, looking to the ocean. "Do something! Help us!"

"Good luck," said Maui. "The ocean doesn't help you; you help yourself!"

Maui rushed to the back of the boat. "Tighten the yard! Bind the stays!" he yelled. Moana stood, confused, and Maui looked at her incredulously. "You can't sail?"

"I . . . uh . . . I am self-taught," said Moana. "Can't you shape-shift or something?"

"You see my hook? Hello?" said Maui. "No hook, no powers!"

The Kakamora took aim and shot their spears

through the air, sinking them into the side of the boat. The spears had ropes tethered to them, and the giant vessel started to reel them in!

The chief knocked on his shell, drumming out another order, and the Kakamora's vessel separated into three!

"Their boat is TURNING INTO MORE BOATS!" said Moana, panicking.

Suddenly, dozens of Kakamora warriors jumped onto the ropes and zip-lined toward them. One by one, Maui pulled the spears out before the coconut bandits could make it across. Meanwhile, Moana struggled, trying with all her might to pull out one of the spears.

Finally, she yanked it from the mast of the ship and smiled smugly at Maui. "Yup, I just did that," she bragged.

Bonk! A Kakamora landed on her head. There was a spear high up on the mast that neither of them had seen! In a flash, the Kakamora army descended on them, knocking Moana to the deck. The heart of Te Fiti fell from her necklace. Moana scrambled for it as it rolled across the hull, but Heihei got to it first and gobbled it up with one peck!

"Heihei!" Moana shouted. The Kakamora grabbed Heihei and raced back up the mast. Moana tried to reach them, but the Kakamora held the rope and cut it, swinging back to their main vessel. "They took the heart!" Moana yelled.

Maui looked at the Kakamora holding Heihei. "That is a chicken."

"The heart's in the—" Moana started, but realized there was no time to explain. "We have to get him back!" she urged.

Two more Kakamora vessels were coming their way. Maui jumped to the other side of the boat, causing it to flip up and sail back toward the main vessel. *"Chee-hoo!"* he yelled.

Moana watched in awe, amazed and impressed by Maui's bold move. She spotted the Kakamora holding Heihei, boarding the main vessel. Moana pointed them out to Maui, but Maui veered to the side. She realized he was not trying to get to Heihei—he was trying to escape!

"What are you doing?" shouted Moana. "The heart!"

"Forget it, you'll never get it back!" said Maui. "Besides, you got a better one." He grinned, holding up the oar he had autographed with a heart and a fishook. Moana grabbed the oar right out of Maui's hands and jumped onto the main vessel as they passed.

"Hey—what am I gonna steer with?" Maui shouted, annoyed. "THEY'RE JUST GONNA KILL YA!" he added, calling after her.

Moana leapt up to a higher level of the vessel and came face to face with a wall of Kakamora. A devious smile crept across her face. "Coconuts...," she said, formulating a plan as she moved.

Whack! She used her oar to bat them aside as she raced across the vessel, knocking down each one in her path. On the other side of the boat, Moana spotted a warrior presenting his chief with Heihei. After whacking more coconuts out of her way, she whizzed by the chief, snatched Heihei, and kept on running.

The Kakamora ran after her, shooting blow darts. One accidentally hit their chief and knocked him unconscious. The guilty warrior shuffled his feet sheepishly as his partner gave him a scolding shove with his elbow.

Gripping her oar in one hand and Heihei in the other, Moana sprinted toward a rope. She put Heihei in her mouth and leapt onto the rope, swinging all the way to the other side of the boat. As more Kakamora warriors approached, she grabbed one of their roped spears and threw it at her boat, sticking it into its side. Then she jumped up and wrapped her oar over the rope. Holding on, she used it to zip-line across, launching herself into the air toward Maui and the canoe.

Moana landed on top of Maui and triumphantly held up Heihei, who puked up the heart. "Got it!" she said proudly, catching the heart in her hand. She looked around and noticed that they were surrounded by Kakamora boats. "Oh."

Maui grabbed the oar and pulled the sail. The Kakamora continued to shoot blow darts at them, but Maui expertly sailed and maneuvered the boat through a small gap. Maui and Moana escaped just in time, the Kakamora boats colliding with each other as they tried to cut off their exit!

"Woo-hoo!" cheered Moana, watching the Kakamora boats sink. "Come on . . . let me hear it. . . ." Moana waited, expecting to hear big compliments from Maui.

"Congratulations on not being dead," Maui said. "You surprised me, Curly," he added warmly. Then he quickly changed his tune. "But I'm still not taking that thing back."

Moana stared at Maui, unwilling to take no for an answer.

"You wanna get to Te Fiti, you gotta go through a whole ocean of bad—not to mention Te Kā," said Maui. "Lava monster? Ever defeat a lava monster?" He showed her his tattoo of Te Kā.

"No," said Moana casually. "Have you?"

Mini Maui winced and gave Moana a check mark on a little tattoo scorecard. Maui looked at Moana, unamused. "I'm not going on a suicide mission with some . . . mortal. You can't restore the heart without me . . . and me says no. I'm getting my hook."

Maui sat down, and Moana looked at him and all of his tattoos, recognizing that the best way to manipulate the demigod was by playing to his giant ego. "You'd be a hero," she said, sitting down next to him as he rifled through her supplies and pulled out a banana. "That's what you're all about, right?"

"Little girl," said Maui, peeling the banana, "I *am* a hero." He took a big bite.

"Maybe you were. . . . But now—now you're just the guy who stole the heart of Te Fiti . . . the guy who cursed the world. You're no one's hero." Moana grabbed the half-eaten banana from Maui and finished it.

Maui scoffed. "No one?" He looked out at the ocean, and it drew up a wave and moved back and forth, as if shaking its head.

Moana held up the heart. "But put the heart back? Save the world? You'd be everyone's hero." Moana whispered in his ear, mimicking the cheer of a crowd, "MAUI, MAUI, MAUI!" As she chanted, Mini Maui and a crowd of tattoos jumped up and down, pretending to be great fans.

Maui got lost in the idea for a moment and then swatted her away like a gnat. "We'd never make it past Te Kā. Not without my hook," he said, dismissing the idea.

"Then we get it," said Moana. "We get your hook, take out Te Kā, restore the heart." She extended her hand. "Unless you don't wanna be Maui, demigod of the wind and sea, hero to . . . all."

Maui considered it and looked at Mini Maui, who was jumping up and down with excitement. Maui placed a finger on him and scooted him onto his back again. "We get my hook first," he said.

Moana nodded. "Then save the world. Deal?" She extended her hand to shake on it.

"Deal." He took Moana's hand and swiftly chucked her overboard. The ocean lifted her right back onto the boat.

Maui shrugged. "Worth a shot."

Chapter 10

Maui put a hand up to the night sky, positioning the stars in the curve of his hand and between his fingers to create a guide. Reading it like a map, he measured the distance between the stars and the horizon. He put his other hand in the ocean to feel the direction of the current. Moana watched, fascinated, as he figured out which way to go.

"We go east, to the lair of Tamatoa," said Maui. "If anyone has my hook, it's that beady-eyed bottom-feeder."

With one mighty pull, Maui filled the sail with

air and the boat jerked, forcing Moana to hang on tightly. Maui swung the sail around and then quickly tied a knot.

Intrigued, Moana watched his every move, eager to learn. "Teach me to sail," she said, inches away from his face.

"Wayfind, princess. What I do is called wayfinding, and it's not just sails and knots; it's seeing where you're going in your mind . . . knowing where you are by knowing where you've been. . . ."

"Okay, first, not a princess. I am the daughter of the chief—"

"Same difference."

"No—"

"If girls want to wear your dress, you're a princess—you are not a wayfinder. You will never be a wayfinder. You will never be a wayfinder," Maui said as if he were stating three separate facts.

Maui picked up Moana and placed her in the cargo hold with Heihei. Then the ocean spit out one of the Kakamora's poisonous darts and sank it right into Maui's butt.

"Really?" Maui said to the ocean. "Blow dart in my butt cheek?"

Maui crumpled to the deck in a heap. Everything but his head was paralyzed. Moana smiled.

"You are a bad person," said Maui, with his face smooshed against the floor of the boat.

"If you can talk, you can teach," said Moana. "Wayfinding, lesson one . . . Hit it."

Maui grunted in protest.

"Untie the halyard," said Maui. Moana chose a rope and began to untie it. "*Not* the halyard," said Maui bluntly. She tried another rope, and Maui said, "Nope." Each rope she tried was the wrong one.

Moments later, Moana stretched her arm up and raised her hand to the sky as she tried to read the stars. She moved her hand back and forth, trying to get it right. "You're measuring stars, not giving the sky a high five," Maui said with disgust.

Moana put her hand in the water. "If the current's warm, you're going the right way," said Maui.

"It's cold. . . . Wait, it's getting warmer!"

Maui cackled.

"Ew, disgusting! What is wrong with you?" said Moana, whipping her hand out of the water.

Moana continued into the night, trying her best to follow Maui's instructions.

The next morning, Moana saw that they were approaching a beautiful green island. "We're here? Maui? See? Told you I could do it!" she said excitedly.

Maui snored. He was fast asleep. Moana looked at the island and realized it was Motunui. "Motunui . . . but . . . I'm home?" she said, confused.

Then, right before her eyes, the lush island turned black, and everything started to shrivel and die. She could see Tui and Sina standing on the island as it deteriorated. They looked terrified and were calling to her for help, but she couldn't get to them.

Moana jerked awake and caught her breath. She looked around, thankful that the whole vision had just been a bad dream.

"Enjoy your beauty rest?" asked Maui sarcastically. The blow dart's effects had finally worn off and he was up and about again. "A real wayfinder never sleeps, so they actually get where they need to go."

A large seabird squawked as it flew overhead, catching Moana's and Maui's attention. They watched as it flapped toward a huge, towering, rock-spired island that stretched into the blue sky.

"Muscle up, buttercup," said Maui. "We're here." The boat reached the rocky shore at the base of the spire, and Maui tied it up.

"You sure this guy's gonna have your hook?" Moana asked.

"Tamatoa? He'll have it. He's a scavenger. Collects stuff, thinks it makes him look cool."

Maui sprinkled a pile of seeds in front of Heihei, still hoping to fatten him up. Heihei pecked away, missing each and every one. Maui placed him in front of a seed and pushed his head down, starting him up like a little toy. Heihei bobbed up and down, pecking at the seed.

"And he lives up there?" asked Moana, staring up at the mile-high spire.

Maui chuckled. "What? Oh no, that's just the entrance. To Lalotai."

"Lalotai? Realm of monsters?" Moana asked nervously. "We're going to the realm of monsters?"

"We? No. Me. You're going to stay here . . . with the other chicken. *Bagock!*" Maui held up a hand to Mini Maui, expecting a high five. "Gimme some," he said. But the tattoo didn't respond. "Nothing?" Giving up, Maui jumped onto the cliff wall and began to climb, talking to Mini Maui along the way. "How do you not get it? I called her a chicken; there's a chicken on the boat. I know she's human, but—never mind, I'm not explaining it to you." Maui eyed Mini Maui and added, "'Cause then it's not funny!"

Moana watched, annoyed, as Maui scaled the spire. She was not about to let him tell her where to stay or what to do. Moana held her necklace close for courage as she prepared to follow Maui to Lalotai.

Chapter 11

Maui made scaling the vertical cliff look simple as he climbed higher and higher. Before long, two hands appeared next to him, straining to keep pace. Maui rolled his eyes when he saw Moana but wasn't surprised that she had followed him. Moana breathed heavily as she jumped to catch rock after rock, pulling herself up the spire.

"So, 'daughter of the chief,'" said Maui as he climbed, "thought you stayed in the village kissing babies. I'm just trying to understand why your people decided to send—um—you."

"My people didn't send me," said Moana, reaching toward another rock. "The ocean did."

"Right. The ocean. Makes sense: you're what . . . eight? Can't sail. Obvious choice."

Moana was aware of Maui's sarcasm. "It chose me for a reason," she said.

"If the ocean's so smart, why didn't it just take the heart back to Te Fiti itself? Or bring me my hook? I'm gonna tell you why, baby face: ocean's kooky-dooks."

Moana looked down to the ocean, now hundreds of feet below. She took a deep breath and continued, focused on making her way to the top.

"But I'm sure it's not wrong about you, right? You're the *Chosen One!*" Maui shoved Moana up the last little bit to help her get to the plateau.

At the top, she looked out at the expansive horizon and closed her eyes. "It chose me for a reason."

"If you start singing, I'm gonna throw up," said Maui as he heaved himself the last few feet to solid ground.

Moana looked around the small, desolate

mountaintop, searching for a way in. "Not seeing an entrance," she said.

"It only appears after a human sacrifice," said Maui. Then he smiled. "Kidding. So serious."

Maui inhaled and let out a heavy breath, blowing dust off the top of the plateau. Then he gave a big warrior cry, stomping his feet dramatically before he jumped onto the rocky ground. It trembled and cracked, revealing a massive face on its surface. The mouth of the face slowly opened, and a strange vortex swirled a thousand feet below. Moana stared at it in awe, completely intimidated.

"Don't worry," said Maui. "It's a lot farther down than it looks." Then he held his knees, jumping in like a cannonball and shouting, *"Cheeeee-hooooo!"*

Moana watched anxiously, frozen for a moment. Then she heard him yell, "I'm still falling!" He finally disappeared into the portal. Moana stared nervously from the ledge as the whirlpool started closing.

"You can do this," she said to herself, willing some confidence. "Go!" she yelled. Without another thought, Moana dove in, and the open mouth slammed shut behind her.

After a long fall, Moana finally hit the ocean waters of the portal and dove deeper and deeper. Her eyes bulged and her vision blurred as she started to run out of air. At the very bottom, a purple spiral swirled supernaturally. In a flash, she was sucked into its depths.

Below her, Maui burst out the floor of the ocean and crashed through the ceiling of the strange underworld. Thunderous growls and groans came out of the fog from enormous monsters lurking in the shadows. Maui landed with effortless grace.

"And he sticks the landing," said Maui, cheering for himself.

He looked at Mini Maui, who smiled as he pulled out a little scoreboard and gave a check to Moana. "What?" said Maui, confused. "Dum-dum, she's not even here. You saw her face; no mortal's gonna jump into—"

Maui stopped midsentence as he watched Moana break into the underworld, right where he had. She smacked into him, bounced off his body, and rolled downhill into a glowing forest made of oddly shaped bioluminescent trees and plants.

"Well, she's dead," Maui said nonchalantly.

Mini Maui gestured for Maui to go help her. But the demigod chose to ignore him.

Moana tried to get her bearings, but she was hanging upside down. Before she knew what was happening, she felt a strange force slowly pulling her up. Then she realized . . . she was wrapped in the tongue of a giant monster! The beast looked like an oversized frog with big lumpy eyes, and Moana was like a little fly trapped in its tongue. The wart-covered monster was slowly but surely slurping her toward its drooling mouth!

As she started to wriggle and panic, an even bigger monster—in the shape of a giant flower—chomped down and ate the first monster in one bite! Luckily, Moana fell to the ground and out of the second monster's reach. But she was still trapped in the slimy severed tongue.

"Ew! Ew! Ew! Ew!" she said, trying to untangle

herself from it.

She quickly ran for cover and peered out to discover a glowing neon world within the mist. Giant anemone trees swayed slowly as sea urchin spines rose up, reaching out, threatening to strike. Creepy sounds and growls echoed all around in a chorus of nightmare terrors. It was the most frightening place Moana had ever been.

"Maui?" Moana whispered urgently, wondering where he had gone. *"Maui?"*

A monster appeared right in front of her and cast a shadow so dark that it blocked out all light and made it impossible for her to see! As it reached for her, it stepped on a small vent that hissed and erupted, shooting out hot, steaming water. The powerful geyser blasted the shadowy monster up into the ocean before he could grab her!

Moana tried to calm herself and realized she was sitting right next to an enormous shell-shaped cave. She peeked inside and could see the unmistakable shape of Maui's magical hook! It was sitting on a pile of shimmering gold and jewels. Maui appeared right behind her and gazed at the giant hook, too.

"Haaaaaaa!" Maui said, yearning to hold it again. He could barely speak, overjoyed to see his prize possession after being separated from it for a very long one thousand years.

Startled by the sound of Maui behind her, Moana turned and instinctively threw a wild punch, right to Maui's gut. He barely flinched and instead just stared at her.

Moana shook her fist, trying to ease the pain in her hand that hitting Maui had caused her. "Sorry, I thought—there was a monst— Earlier there was a big, horrible— But I found your hook, so that's goo—" she stammered, trembling with fear.

Maui palmed her head and picked her up, placing her to the side of the cave. "Stay here. Be quiet," he whispered.

"What? No," Moana said, starting to follow.

"'Cause *you're* gonna face Tamatoa?" Maui asked sarcastically with raised eyebrows. "I've been waiting a thousand years to get my hook, and it's gonna be hard enough without it getting screwed up by a mortal, who has no business being in a monster cave except . . . ," Maui's voice trailed off as a plan brewed. His eyes brightened when he came up with an idea. "Except maybe as bait."

Moana's face fell, but before she could protest, Maui put her to work.

As if clanging cymbals together, Moana banged a pile of gold objects noisily as she made her way through the treasure-filled lair. A variety of jewels and treasures were strewn all over, making every corner of the place sparkle and glimmer.

Moana took a deep breath as she prepared to play her part. "Wow," she said, sounding stiff and overly loud. "There is a *lot* of shiny stuff in here!"

"Louder," Maui whispered from behind a big mound of gold.

"Gold, gold, gold!" shouted Moana, a little louder. "I love gold!"

Moana walked around the lair, tripping over jewels and continuing to make as much noise as she could.

Maui remained hidden and whispered to her,

"When he shows up, keep him distracted; get him to talk about himself. You know the type—loves bragging about how great he is."

"You two must get along great," said Moana.

"Not since I ripped off his leg," said Maui. "Although with that guy, it's really more of an arm. He's got plenty."

"Of arms?" asked Moana, starting to feel nervous. "How many does he have? Maui? Hello? *Hello?*"

But Maui was gone. Suddenly, the pile of treasures behind Moana rumbled and rose. She braced herself, ready to meet Tamatoa.

Chapter 12

"**H**ello," said a sinister voice.

The ground beneath Moana's feet shook, and she turned to see a fifty-foot crab monster staring at her! The sparkling gold and jewels were all piled up and calcified, hardened onto the back of his enormous shell. He snatched Moana in one of his pincers and held her up to his creepy face. She screamed in terror, but Tamatoa covered her mouth and rudely said, "Mute that!" He looked her up and down and said, "Little human, whoa-ho-ho . . . in the realm of monsters." His protruding eyes circled her, checking her out from every angle as Moana followed them fearfully. "Well—pick an eye, babe. I can't concentrate on what I'm saying when you're going back and forth like—Just pick one," he said as she looked at one of his eyestalks and then at the other one. "Pick *one*," he demanded. As Moana tried to focus on only one of his eyes, he asked, "What are you doing down here, *human*?"

He flipped her in the air to get a better hold on her, and Moana could see Maui attempting to sneak around behind Tamatoa. Maui silently motioned to Moana, wanting to remind her of the plan to get Tamatoa to talk about himself, but it was clear that Moana did not want to go that route. When Tamatoa turned one eyeball to see what Moana was looking at, Maui was gone.

"I, uh . . . I love your shell," said Moana awkwardly, trying to follow Maui's idea.

"Everyone loves my shell, *mon poisson*. It's spectacular," Tamatoa said nonchalantly. "But you didn't answer my query." He used a jagged claw to poke threateningly at Moana. Behind him, Moana could see Maui sneaking forward, closer to them.

"Why are you here?" Tamatoa asked sharply as he fiddled with Moana's necklace.

"Don't! That's my gramma's," Moana said, swatting at him with her hands.

"'That's my gramma's,'" Tamatoa said, rudely mimicking her. "I ate my grandparents. *Why are you here?*" he asked, louder. He pulled her in even closer, and she shrank back in fear.

She peered behind Tamatoa and could see Maui moving toward them.

Tamatoa raised his voice, demanding an answer from her as he leaned in. "Why are you—"

"To rob you!" Moana blurted. "I came to—to steal one of your treasures. But now, in the presence . . . of your . . . splendor . . . ," Moana said hesitantly, searching for the right words. "I just—I honestly just want to know how you became so beautiful."

Tamatoa stared at Moana for a beat, looking at her skeptically. "Are you trying to get me to talk about myself?" he asked. Moana looked at him, unsure of how to react. But to her surprise, he flashed a big eerie smile and said, "Why didn't you say so?"

The monstrous crab struck a pose and bragged about all the shiny stuff on his back. Maui was right; Tamatoa was more than happy to chat about himself and told her he liked feeling beautiful. He explained that his obsession with decorating his shell with treasures was practical, too: he never had to look for fish to eat because they were lured in by all his glittering gold. He demonstrated by eating a whole bunch of fish. They had been hypnotized by his shell and had swum down to the bottom of the ocean. Then they had fallen into the realm of monsters, and Tamatoa's mouth.

Tamatoa flipped Moana up into the air. From there, she could see Maui struggling to climb toward his fishhook.

Tamatoa caught her in midair and then dangled her over his mouth as he eyed her hungrily. He was already prepared for his next meal. Moana panicked as she searched for Maui . . . but he had disappeared! Tamatoa brought her closer to his teeth, and just as the giant crab monster was about to chomp down on her, Maui leapt in and grabbed his hook, yanking it from the shell.

He hurried to Moana and scooped her up, then posed like a superhero, feeling like he was on top of the world. "It's okay, you're safe now," Maui said.

Moana smiled gratefully . . . until she realized Maui was talking to his hook.

"Whaddaya say, little buddy?" Maui asked, looking to Mini Maui for a suggestion. Mini Maui transformed into a hawk. "Giant hawk? Comin' up! *Chee-hoo!*" shouted Maui as he triumphantly held the hook above his head. It glowed and flashed brightly, and he transformed into a . . . fish. Maui tried again, but he transformed into a bug, then a pig . . . then he was back to being a demigod.

Tamatoa stared at Maui, wondering what was wrong. Maui shook his hook a little, attempting to fix it. He tried a third time, but his shape-shifting powers were just not working. The demigod was getting more and more frustrated.

Tamatoa sneered, thoroughly enjoying Maui's predicament. He moved toward Maui and knocked him across the cave with one of his giant legs. When Maui pulled himself up, Tamatoa hit him again.

"Stop it!" yelled Moana, shocked by his violent force.

His attention returned to Moana, and Tamatoa tossed her into a makeshift cage made out of whale and fish bones. Then he continued to torture and mock Maui, not noticing when Moana managed to slip through the slats of the bone cage. She looked around for a way out and spotted a crack in the cave's wall leading outside. Moana glanced back to see Maui getting beaten up and knew she couldn't leave him.

As he poked and prodded Maui, Tamatoa talked more about himself and his love of collecting shiny things. He grabbed Maui's hook and jammed it back into his shell. Then he pushed Maui to the ground. Using the sharp, jagged edge of his torn claw, he cut into a tattoo of a woman and baby on Maui's back. Maui tried with all his might to push Tamatoa off, but he seemed paralyzed by the crab monster's force.

Tamatoa laughed wickedly and tossed Maui against the wall of the cave, pinning him there with one of his pincers. As he prepared to end Maui's life with a final blow, Moana called to him. "I've got something shiny for ya!" She held up the glowing heart to get Tamatoa's attention.

"The heart of Te Fiti," Tamatoa said eagerly.

Holding the heart, Moana ran off. Desperate for the elusive treasure, Tamatoa instantly dropped Maui to chase her. Maui watched, stunned, as Tamatoa gained on her. Moana lost her footing, tripped, and dropped the heart. It rolled and fell down into a crevice!

As Tamatoa rushed toward the crevice, Moana ran up his shell and grabbed Maui's hook! She jumped down and dragged the heavy fishhook to Maui as Tamatoa tried to get to the heart.

Moana noticed the cut in the tattoo on Maui's

back and wondered if he was okay, but she knew there was no time to ask. "We gotta go," she said, eyeing Tamatoa as he continued to dig into the crevice.

"But the heart . . . ," said Maui.

"He can have it," whispered Moana. She revealed the heart inside her shell necklace and smiled. "I've got a better one."

It was then that Tamatoa finally pulled out what he thought was the heart . . . but it was only a nasty old barnacle covered with glowing green seaweed. He instantly knew he had been tricked, and he was furious.

"Come on! Run!" shouted Moana, taking off.

Full of rage, Tamatoa charged at them, his claws rapidly tapping against the ground as he ran faster and faster. Moana quickly ducked, and Tamatoa smashed into the wall, knocking a hole into it. As Moana pulled Maui through and out of the cave, he transformed into a fish. Moana picked him up and carried him as she continued to run from Tamatoa. But without warning, Maui transformed back to his normal form, and she dropped him! Right behind them, Tamatoa reared up, ready to attack. Moana yanked Maui onto a geyser hole— and it hissed and erupted just in the nick of time, lifting them out of Tamatoa's reach!

The force knocked Tamatoa back on his shell, and he was stuck, like a turtle. His glittering treasures cracked off and spilled all around as he flailed helplessly.

"*Chee-hoo!*" shouted Moana. The mighty geyser blew them straight up through the ceiling of the underworld and back into the arms of the ocean!

Chapter 13

Moana and Maui shot through the water while Maui continued to randomly transform into a variety of figures. When they finally burst through to the other side, they crashed down into the shallow water beside the spire island.

"*Whoo!*" shouted Moana triumphantly. "We're alive, we're al—*AAAGH!*"

Moana turned to Maui, who had only half transformed. Now he had his normal body but the head of a huge shark!

"Listen," started shark-headed Maui, "I appreciate

what you did down there, took guts, but, uh—"

Moana nodded blankly. "Mm-hm, mm-hm, mm-hm." She was trying to listen but was having a hard time taking the strange talking shark head seriously.

"Sorry, I'm trying to be sincere for once, and it feels like you're distracted," said Maui.

"No, nope," Moana said coolly.

Maui stared at her suspiciously through his shark eyes. "You're looking at me like I have a . . ." He sighed, finally realizing. "Shark head."

"Do you have a shark head?" Moana asked, trying to keep a straight face. "'Cause I didn't even—"

"Agh! Just . . . the point is, for a little girl . . . child . . . who had no business down there, you did me a solid. . . . *But* you also almost died . . . and I couldn't even beat that dumb crab. So chances of beating Te Kā? Bupkis. This mission is cursed."

"It's not cursed," said Moana.

"Shark head," said Maui, proving a point.

"It is *not* cursed," said Moana.

She lifted Maui's hook and placed it in his little

flippers. The hook flashed, and he zapped back to his normal form. Moana smiled, but then Maui continued to uncontrollably transform into a series of different animals as his hook flashed and zapped.

He went from being a pig to a fish to a bug to a whale in the blink of an eye. Once he finally stopped changing form, his top half was back to normal, but his bottom half was shark.

"Cursed," said Maui, standing up on his shark fins and looking at Moana with a deadpan expression.

Moments later, Moana and Maui were on the boat, feeling beaten down and exhausted. Maui had his hair wrapped up on top of his head in a bun and was somberly lying on his back. Moana looked down at the heart of Te Fiti inside her necklace, trying to figure out what to do next.

Maui, feeling hopeless and depressed, sang a strange-sounding tune to himself. "Hey, what can I say? Te Kā's gonna kill us, gonna kill us . . ."

"Can you at least try?" asked Moana, attempting to get him back on track.

Maui put a lazy finger on his hook and fritzed a few more times, changing into a variety of forms before turning back to his normal self. He started to sing again, this time louder. "Hey! Today's our last day. Te Kā's gonna kill us, gonna kill us."

Unable to put up with any more of Maui's negativity, Moana poked him in the side with the oar. "All right—break time's over. Get up," she ordered.

"Why?" asked Maui. "You gonna gimme a speech? Tell me I can beat Te Kā 'cause I'm Maui?"

Mini Maui protested Maui's attitude with a stomp and scowl.

"Take a hike," Maui said to the little tattoo. He pushed him over his shoulder. As Moana watched Mini Maui move to Maui's back, she spotted the tattoo of the woman holding the baby that Tamatoa had been digging into.

"How do you get your tattoos?" Moana asked.

"They show up . . . when I earn 'em," Maui replied.

"How'd you earn that one?" asked Moana. "What's that for?"

Maui glanced back, noticing the one she was asking about. "That tattoo is man's discovery of Nunya."

"What's Nunya?"

"Nunya business."

Maui tried to lie back down, and Moana knocked him with her oar. "I'll just keep asking. What's it for?"

Maui didn't respond, and Moana whacked him again.

"You need to stop doing that," said Maui.

Moana paused for a moment, then reached out with the oar and tapped him on his man bun. "How'd you get the tattoo?" she asked.

When he didn't answer, she gave him another whack.

"Back off," Maui said, his irritation growing.

Moana hit him with the oar again. "Tell me what it is," she insisted.

"I said *back off.*"

She whacked him again. "Is it why your hook's not working? 'Cause—"

Fed up, Maui spun around and knocked Moana into the water, hard. Moana floated there, staring up at Maui in surprise. He looked down at his hook, embarrassed by what he had done, but he still felt angry.

He walked to the other side of the boat. Moana studied Maui for a moment, and then she climbed back in. She stared at him, trying to figure out what to do and say.

"You don't wanna talk. Don't talk," she said, trying to converse with him as he sat with his back facing her. "You wanna throw me off the boat, throw me off. You wanna—you wanna tell me I don't know what I'm doing? I know I don't. I have no idea why the ocean chose me. You're right. But I came anyway. . . . My people don't even go past the reef. . . . But I am here . . . for you . . . and I want to help, but I can't if you don't let me."

Moana looked at Maui, who sat silently, as if ignoring her. She started to turn away, but he began to speak.

"I wasn't born a demigod . . ."

Moana stopped and listened as Maui turned toward her.

"I was born human. My parents were human. They, uh, they took one look . . . and decided . . . they did not want me. They threw me into the sea. A baby. Like I was nothing."

Moana looked at his tattoo and realized the lady pictured was Maui's mother, tossing him away.

"Somehow I was found by the gods. They gave me the hook." He gestured to his hook sitting on the edge of the boat. "*They* made me Maui. And back to the humans I went. . . . They needed islands, fire . . . coconuts. Anything they could ever want. There I was." Maui looked out at the water, lost in his memory, lost in sharing his story. "And they loved me. I was Maui . . . the Great Maui."

He turned and looked at Moana. She could see a deep sadness in his eyes and felt sympathy for him. Feeling vulnerable, Maui quickly looked away.

Moana eyed the tattoo of him being thrown into the sea. "Maybe the gods found you for a reason," she said gently. "Maybe the ocean brought you to them because it saw someone who deserved to be saved." Moana looked out at the rolling waves and then turned back to Maui. "The gods aren't the ones who make you Maui. You are."

Maui let her words wash over him and sink in as he tried to hide his emotions, uncomfortable with having revealed so much about himself. "Pretty good speech," he said. He looked down to see Mini Maui giving him a hug. Maui hugged him back. "Okay, now it's weird. Let's get to work."

Moana and Mini Maui helped him return to training, and this time Maui got better. He practiced using his hook and improved his skills, working hard to become stronger and stronger. Soon, Maui gained control of his shape-shifting powers and was able to transform as he wished.

Feeling confident, he turned into a giant hawk and slashed with his hook to cut a cliff in half. He landed on the boat and gave Moana a triumphant fist bump, thrilled to feel like his old self again.

Then Maui picked up the oar and offered it to Moana. The time had come for him to willingly teach her, so that she could become a master wayfinder. She was surprised and hesitated, but Maui nodded his head, holding the oar out to her, insisting. Moana smiled and accepted, feeling truly honored. She gripped the oar, more than ready to learn how to wayfind.

Chapter 14

Maui reached his hand to the sky to read the stars, and Moana raised her hand, too. Maui lifted her arm a little higher, placing it in just the right spot, showing her the proper way to navigate.

A moon bow shone brightly above as the ocean carried their little boat into the night.

With a little help from Maui, Moana managed to lead the way, navigating using the stars and the moon. He was proud of how well she did and believed she was well on her way to being a great wayfinder.

As dawn broke and a bright sun rose over the horizon, Maui sat perched on the mast of the boat, looking out through the haze. He watched Moana for a moment as she guided the boat, appreciating her skills. Then he looked back out at the sea, deep in thought. He turned to Moana and smiled.

"What?" Moana asked curiously.

"I figured it out," Maui said, grinning. He jumped down to the deck of the boat, landing on both feet with a great thud. "The ocean used to love when I pulled up islands . . . 'cause your ancestors would sail her seas to find 'em. All those new lands . . . the people . . . it was the water that connected them all. And if I were the ocean, I think I'd be looking for a curly-haired non-princess to start that again."

"That is the nicest thing you've ever said to me," said Moana. "Probably should've saved it for Te Fiti," she added playfully.

Maui smiled. "I did."

Maui gestured out over the boat. As the haze began to lift, Moana saw something in the distance. Beyond the rolling swells of the ocean, she could make out a clear ring of islands rising up out of the water. They created a barrier to Te Fiti. The great island goddess was resting within their protection. Moana couldn't believe it . . . they had actually made it.

"Moana of Motunui, I believe you have officially delivered Maui across the great sea," Maui said. Then he turned to Mini Maui and said, "Round of applause."

Mini Maui cheered, and a group of tattoo figures bobbed up and down as Maui imitated the roar of a crowd. "Haaaa . . . Moanaaaa . . . you're so amazing."

Moana chuckled, and the two looked at each other with pride, feeling good about how far they had come.

"It's time," Maui said, holding his hand out to her.

As Moana pulled the heart of Te Fiti from her shell necklace, a deafening, high-pitched noise broke the silence. Clouds of smoke and ash began to build.

Moana handed him the heart and said, "Go save the world."

Maui took the heart and his magical hook. Then he transformed into a hawk. Flapping his mighty wings, he rocketed toward the rough waters around the barrier islands.

Moana cheered him on. As he approached the plumes of ash, a horrific face appeared through the clouds: Te Kā. The molten monster screamed and shrieked with rage as it revealed itself. It was the size of a mountain and grew as it moved, reaching up into the sky. Te Kā dripped with lava and flashed with the fires of Earth's inner forces. It was a terrifying sight.

"Maui . . . ," said Moana, her body stiffening with fear.

Before Maui could even react, Te Kā knocked him hard, and his powers fritzed. He shook it off and flew higher and higher. Te Kā raised a molten fist and, with one ferocious swipe, knocked Maui from the sky.

"No!" Moana screamed.

As Maui plummeted toward the ocean, Moana filled her sail and raced to try and catch him. Maui hit the water hard, but Moana snatched him up as she sailed past. Then she ran back to the oar and started to steer toward a gap in the barrier islands.

"Wh-what are you doing?" asked Maui, confused.

"Finding you a better way in!" she said. She slalomed the boat and was lined up to break through the barrier islands, but Te Kā was approaching fast.

"We won't make it!" shouted Maui. He grabbed the oar and tried to take control of the canoe. "TURN AROUND! STOP! MOANA, STOP!" he shouted.

Determined, Moana ignored him and continued to steer the boat, dead set on succeeding in their mission. Te Kā was gaining on them, racing faster and faster. When the monster was a few feet away, Maui shoved Moana, knocking her aside with the oar. But it was too late. Te Kā's fist came down toward her. At the last second, Maui raised his hook high in the air to block it.

As Te Kā hit Maui's hook, a huge shock wave rippled out, causing ocean swells that blasted Moana and Maui farther from Te Fiti. Te Kā lunged over the top of the waves, trying to reach them, but couldn't. It was as if Te Kā was tethered to the barrier islands. The enormous tidal surge continued to carry Moana and Maui, pushing them into the darkness.

Chapter 15

When the water finally calmed, Moana picked herself up off the hull and saw the damaged canoe. The sail was torn and the sides of the boat were cracked. She felt terrible, knowing it was all her fault, and looked around for Maui, fearing the worst. She spotted him and called out with great relief, "Maui! Oh, thank— You're okay!"

Maui slowly turned, revealing his hook. A deep crack cut through the center of it from one end to the other. Moana's heart sank.

"I told you to turn back," he said softly.

"Maui . . . I'm . . . ," Moana whispered.

Maui finally lifted his eyes to hers, and she could see how upset he was. She looked down at the fractured hook. "We can fix it," she said.

"It was made by the gods! You can't fix it."

"Next time, we'll be more careful. Te Kā was stuck on the barrier islands. . . . It's lava; it can't go in the water. We can find a way around."

Maui stared at Moana, incredulous. "I'm not going back," he said firmly.

"You still have to restore the heart."

"My hook is cracked. One more hit, and it's over."

"Maui, you have to restore the heart," Moana said, unwilling to give up.

"Without my hook, I'm nothing."

"Maui—"

"WITHOUT MY HOOK, I AM *NOTHING*!" his voice boomed.

Maui's anger took Moana's breath away, and she stared at him, speechless. He dropped the heart of Te Fiti onto the hull of the boat.

"Maui . . . ," Moana said as he pushed past her, "we're only here because you stole the heart in the first place."

"We're here because I keep listening when humans beg for my help. And I'm done."

Moana picked up the heart of Te Fiti and faced Maui, standing strong. Determined, she started her speech once again. "I am Moana of Motunui, you will board my boat—"

"Goodbye, Moana," Maui said, interrupting her, unwilling to listen.

"Sail across the sea—"

"I'm not killing myself so you can prove you're something you're not—"

"And restore the heart of Te Fiti!" she said desperately, holding up the heart, waving it at him. "The ocean chose me!" she cried.

Maui turned away. "It chose wrong," he said. Then without another word, he transformed into a hawk and jumped up into the sky. Flapping his giant wings, he took off.

"Maui? *Maui!*" yelled Moana, watching him

disappear into the darkness.

All alone, Moana looked down at the heart, now scratched and covered with ash. She touched its spiral with her finger and felt a rush of emotions. She couldn't believe it was all over. She had come so far and tried so hard, but she had failed.

Under twinkling stars above, she looked out at the ocean. Its dark, rippling waves quietly stretched out as far as she could see. Moana had never felt so disappointed in herself. She stood on the boat as it bobbed to the beat of the waves, feeling empty and alone.

The ocean slowly drew up a small wave that faced her. "Why did you bring me here?" she asked, her eyes full of sadness. "He's gone; you chose the wrong person." She held the heart out. "You have to choose someone else. Choose someone else! CHOOSE SOMEONE ELSE!" Moana's voice dropped as she said, "Please . . ."

In the light of the moon, the ocean reached up and gently surrounded Moana's hand. It took the heart, letting it float for only a moment. Moana watched as the heart slowly sank and disappeared once again, swallowed up by the sea.

Moana stood motionless. Overwhelmed by her failure, she fell to her knees at the bow of the boat and wept. With tears in her eyes, she looked down at the empty necklace and thought about Gramma Tala. The memory of her made Moana feel even worse.

Suddenly, a glimmer appeared far off on the horizon. It streaked through the dark ocean, racing toward her. The light rocketed under her boat, and she could see that it was a spectral manta ray. Moana watched as the beautiful ray effortlessly flapped its great fins, circling the canoe. Then, without warning, it vanished.

"You're a long way past the reef," said a familiar voice. Moana turned to see Gramma Tala sitting on the bow of the boat!

"Gramma?"

"Well, you just gonna sit there?" Gramma Tala asked.

"Gramma!" Moana said, stumbling across the

boat to reach her. She fell into her gramma's arms. "I tried, Gramma. I—I couldn't make it. . . ."

Gramma Tala wiped Moana's tears. "It's not your fault. I never should have put so much on your shoulders. If you are ready to go home . . . I will be with you."

Moana nodded and reached for her oar. She lifted it up, but as she went to dip it in the water . . . she stopped. She stared at the oar, feeling confused and uncertain.

"Why do you hesitate?" asked Gramma Tala.

"I don't know," said Moana, tearing up again. She didn't know what to do. She couldn't hear her voice inside and feared it might be gone forever.

Gramma Tala told her that her voice was always there; she only had to listen. Moana thought about her family and her island, the things she loved most. She recalled all she had been through and reflected on everything she had learned on her journey. She remembered finding Maui, learning to wayfind, and fighting off scary monsters in a strange underworld. She realized the history of where she was from, and her voyaging ancestors inspired her. As she continued to think of those strong, fearless ancestors, their ghostly images appeared in large ocean-voyaging canoes before her, encouraging her to continue on her quest.

As Moana looked into the sea, contemplating everything and listening to Gramma Tala's wisdom, she heard a tiny voice inside herself again. She dug down deep, listening hard for it, and it became louder and stronger.

As she leaned over the side of the boat, she caught sight of the heart, far below the waves, glowing on the ocean floor, and she knew exactly who she was and what she had to do.

Feeling empowered, Moana dove off the side of the boat and swam down into the darkness, deeper and deeper, searching for the heart of Te Fiti. Just as she was about to run out of air, she reached the heart and grabbed it. She clutched it tightly, and the ocean pushed her through the water at lightning speed until she surfaced. When she got back on the boat, Gramma Tala and the ancestors were gone.

The night was silent when Moana resurfaced . . . she was all alone. But she knew what she had to do now, and she was determined.

Moana repaired the damaged canoe, sewing the sail and mending its cracked sides. As she worked, she repeated to herself, "I am Moana of Motunui. Aboard my boat, I will sail across the sea . . . and restore the heart of Te Fiti!"

Reinvigorated, and feeling more determined than ever, Moana tightened a line, swung the boom, filled the sail, and took off toward Te Fiti.

Chapter 16

Using her wayfinding skills, Moana sailed into the morning. As her boat rode over huge rolling swells, she spotted the ring of barrier islands surrounding Te Fiti in the distance. When she approached, she found a gap wide enough for her canoe to pass through.

"Te Kā can't follow us into the water. . . . We make it past the barrier islands . . . we make it to Te Fiti." She put Heihei in a basket. "None of which you understand because you are a chicken."

Moana gripped the heart and prepared herself

as she sailed toward the small opening. Through a thick cloud of ash, she could see the bright fires of Te Kā.

Moana eased the boat forward. Te Kā roared as it emerged, rising up and covering half the sky. It spit and spewed hot lava and raised a massive fist, about to destroy the boat, but Moana was ready. Using one of Maui's tricks, she jumped on the boat to make it flip up on its side and then headed toward a second gap, managing to escape Te Kā's violent blow.

Fueled by even more anger, Te Kā screeched as it raced across the barrier islands at full speed, trying to cut Moana off. The ferocious volcano monster hurled chunks of molten lava, which exploded in huge plumes of ash and steam as they hit the water with an angry hiss. Moana slalomed the boat to avoid the lava and made her way closer and closer to the pass.

But Te Kā was too fast for Moana and blocked the opening with lava. When the steam cleared, Moana was nowhere to be found. Te Kā's flaming head whipped right to left, scouring the area, hunting for her. To the monster's surprise, Moana appeared out of reach, unfurling her sail. She had doubled back and was rocketing toward the first gap!

Te Kā shrieked with rage and threw a gigantic ball of lava. It smashed into the mountains above Moana. She pulled the line hard and sliced through the gap, but enormous boulders crashed down, falling all around her. Moana lost her grip on the rope, but to her surprise, Heihei grabbed it just before it slipped away! Moana took the rope and made it through the barrier islands!

"We did it!" Moana shouted. "We—" She turned to smile at Heihei but realized he wasn't on the boat. He was flailing in the water behind her. "Heihei?"

Unable to leave the rooster behind, she thrust her oar into the water to stop and spun her boat around. She sailed toward Heihei and plucked him out of the sea. Just as she was about to continue sailing toward Te Fiti, a deafening noise blared as the mighty volcano monster emerged once again, snarling and growling. The force of Te Kā's movement sent a sky-high wave toward Moana, and her boat didn't stand a chance. It capsized and Moana was tossed into the water!

As boulders rained down, Moana swam toward the canoe and tried to flip it, but she was not strong enough to pull it up. Te Kā raised a fist to deliver a hefty blow, but a moment before it hit, there was a loud screeching noise and a flash of white light. A giant hawk knocked Te Kā's hand away just in time. Maui had returned!

He resumed his demigod form and smiled at Moana.

"Maui?" She couldn't believe he had come to help her. "But your hook . . . ?"

Maui lifted his magical hook and used it to flip her boat back over. Then he looked at Mini Maui. "Yeah, well, we were talking about what you said . . . well, it's funny, I realized I *am* the only one who can make me, me."

Behind him, Te Kā rose up again.

"Mm-hm, mm-hm, mm-hm," said Moana, trying

to wrap it up. "Maui, there's . . . uh, Maui . . ."

Maui continued to ramble on about his feelings. "Do I have abandonment and self-worth issues? Yes, I do. Also some latent narcissism and—"

"Maui!" Moana screamed as a fireball flew right by them. Te Kā loomed above.

"Right. Another time— I got your back, Chosen One. Go save the world," said Maui as he turned toward Te Kā.

"Maui!" Moana shouted again. "Thank you."

Maui glanced at Moana with a sincere smile and said, "You're welcome."

Taking a deep breath, Maui channeled his energy, transformed into a hawk, and flew toward Te Kā. Once he was over the lava monster, he transformed into a lizard. "Hot-hot-hot-hot-hot!" he said, scurrying over the monster's fiery arm.

Standing strong at the helm of her boat, Moana unfurled the sail and dodged lava, handling the boat like she never had before. As Moana headed closer to Te Fiti, Maui cheered her on as he slipped between Te Kā's fingers and then turned into a hawk . . . until Te Kā knocked him out of the sky! When Maui hit the ground of the barrier islands, he transformed back into a demigod as the crack in his hook grew. But that no longer mattered. Maui saw Te Kā holding up a lava ball, aiming for Moana, and knew what he had to do. He wielded his hook and, with all his might, smashed it into Te Kā, distracting it from Moana.

Moana docked her boat and raced up the shore of Te Fiti to put the heart back. A blinding explosion lit up the sky behind her as Maui slammed down to the ground with a thunderous boom. His hook smashed into the rocky surface beside him and shattered into pieces.

As Moana scrambled to reach the top of the hill, she suddenly stopped, confused. She frowned as she lifted her head and looked around desperately. Something was very wrong.

"No . . . ," she said, feeling a tightening in her chest. She couldn't believe her eyes.

Of all the things Moana had been expecting, she had never imagined this. There was supposed to be an island beyond the hill, but instead, there was a hollow shell with . . . nothing in the center.

Te Fiti wasn't there. Only an empty crater stretched before her. There was nowhere to put the heart. "Te Fiti . . . she's gone. . . ."

Chapter 17

Maui continued to fight Te Kā, even without his hook. "Come on! COME ON!" he yelled at the lava monster.

No longer sure what to do, Moana took a deep breath to calm herself and listened for her voice inside. She turned and saw Te Kā looming over Maui, volcanic lightning flashing all around them. And then she spotted something on Te Kā's chest. A glowing spiral covered up by cooling lava. Moana looked over her shoulder at the empty crater where Te Fiti should be.

"The spiral . . . ," she said, looking down at the heart in her hand. Its glow brightened with her every step and she looked to the ocean. Moana knew what she had to do.

As Te Kā lifted a mighty fist to destroy Maui, a blinding light glowed from the heart. Moana held it above her head like a beacon, shining brighter and brighter. Te Kā noticed the light and turned its eyes toward it.

"Let her come to me," Moana said to the ocean. And the ocean began to recede and part, like it had so many years ago when Moana was a toddler on the beach. As she walked along the path, the water continued to part . . . opening a channel all the way to Te Kā's barrier islands.

"Moana! What are you doing?" shouted Maui.

Te Kā, full of fury, raced down the open channel toward Moana and the heart! But Moana walked peacefully and deliberately toward Te Kā. She looked directly at the raging monster and sang to it calmly, completely focused on it. Moana reminded the monster that there was still a voice down deep inside that no one could ever take away. She explained that she knew what it was like to lose that little voice, and she encouraged the monster to listen to its own.

As Te Kā listened to Moana's words, the lava monster became quiet and calm. It soon came to rest at Moana's feet. Moana reached out and put the heart of Te Fiti into the spiral on Te Kā's chest and whispered, "Know who you are."

Te Kā closed its eyes, and suddenly its rocky exterior cracked open and crumbled apart, revealing a beautiful, serene green face. Te Kā *was* Te Fiti! A vibrant crown of flowers and leaves bloomed around Te Fiti's head.

Maui watched in complete shock as Te Fiti rose and the ocean lifted Moana up into the air. Without warning, Maui was also grabbed by the ocean, sucked under, and dragged to the shore. He was placed right next to Moana. The ocean then carried Heihei and deposited him beside them, too.

"The chicken lives!" shouted Maui, looking at Heihei.

The ground rumbled and shook as Te Fiti used her hand to lift Moana and Maui up toward her face.

Moana knelt and pulled Maui down to his knees, too. Te Fiti nodded in gratitude to Moana, and Moana nodded back. Then Te Fiti looked at Maui . . . who shrugged, embarrassed.

"Hey there, Te Fiti. So . . . how ya been . . . ?" Maui said, trying to be charming. Te Fiti stared at him, unimpressed, and Maui looked down at his feet. "Look, what I did was . . . I have no excuse. I did it for myself and . . . and I'm sorry." Maui looked up sincerely.

Te Fiti raised her fist and waited just a moment before opening it. In her palm was Maui's magical hook. Maui couldn't believe it—it was fixed and looked as beautiful as it had the day he'd gotten it!

"YES! *Chee-hoo!*" he said, overjoyed. He stopped himself and lowered his voice, trying to remain respectful. "Thank you, uh, thank you . . . your kind gesture is deeply, deeply appreciated." He added a small, *"Chee-hoo!"* Then he turned into a tiny bug and flew off.

Te Fiti lifted Moana close and gave her a *hongi*. She lowered Moana next to Maui on the shore and faded into the island as blossoms exploded all around them. A sea of pink petals floated through the air, swirling onto the sand over Moana's boat, now fully restored and decorated with bright, beautiful flowers!

Maui scattered some birdseed for Heihei. "Gonna miss ya, Drumstick," he said. Heihei tried to eat the food but missed. Maui smiled fondly and shook his head. "Don't ever change."

Maui looked at Moana, and they both knew it was almost time to say goodbye. Moana gazed out to the ocean. "You could come with us, you know," she said. "My people are going to need a master wayfinder."

"They already have one," said Maui.

He smiled as a new tattoo appeared over his heart. It was a picture of Moana, the proud wayfinder. Mini Maui smiled at Moana, then lifted the sky of the particular tattoo he was in and comfortably settled into place.

Moana jumped up and pulled Maui in for a big hug. When they parted, Maui swung his hook mightily, charging up and turning into a hawk. With one last smile, he flew off into the sky.

Moana hoisted her sail and glanced back at the island of Te Fiti, awash with color. She dipped her oar into the water and headed out to sea.

Chapter 18

The black, dying plants across the island of Motunui suddenly sprang to life. An explosion of green foliage and colorful flowers circled Sina and Tui. Sina took one look at the vibrant plants and raced for the shore. Tui dropped an armful of supplies and followed, running to catch up. From the water's edge, they could make out a boat in the distance.

Moana's canoe blasted over the ocean's whitecaps as it sped toward the lush green peaks of Motunui. Moana soared over the reef. When she got close enough, she jumped out of the boat and ran up to her parents. Sina grabbed her and wrapped Moana in her arms. With tears in his eyes, Tui hugged Moana tightly. The family held each other for a long moment, happy to be reunited.

"I may have gone a *little* way past the reef," Moana said.

Tui smiled and looked at the boat. "Suits you," he said with a nod.

Soon the villagers joined them on the shore, and Pua excitedly rushed over to Moana, nuzzling against her and covering her with kisses. "Pua! Whoa, snout in the mouth!"

As Moana played with Pua, a pack of village kids raced past and leapt onto Moana's canoe, pretending to be wayfinders.

Days later, the whole village pulled the huge double-hulled, ocean-voyaging canoes out of the cavern. Moana smiled proudly as she gazed at the boats of her ancestors. The ocean spiraled at her feet, and a little wave carried her conch shell, washing it onto the shore. Moana knelt down and picked up the beautiful, sparkling pink shell. Taking a walk, she placed the shell at the very top of the highest peak in Motunui, raising the island higher, just like her father and his father before him.

It wasn't long before the villagers stood at the water's edge, cheering a fleet of departing canoes, led by Moana. Tui and Sina raced next to her, on their own boat. Tui pulled a rope and their huge canoe passed Moana's. She quickly maneuvered her sail and rocketed to the front of the fleet, looking back at her parents proudly.

As she leaned out on the outrigger, a spectral manta ray swam beneath her and she smiled, knowing it was Gramma Tala.

In the sky above, a massive hawk screeched as it dove toward Moana, slicing the water and creating a wake for her to jump. Her canoe crested the swell and landed smoothly, gliding across the water. Standing confidently at the helm of her boat, Moana—the wayfinder, the warrior, the next great chief of her people—knew she was exactly where she was meant to be.